THE TWELVE-
HEADED GRIFFIN
&
OTHER STORIES

Publications from
The Scheherazade Foundation

The Secrets of Scheherazade
An Ordered Experience
Tale of a Lantern & Other Stories
The Elephant & The Tortoise & Other Stories
The Monkey's Fiddle & Other Stories
Ghost of the Violet Well & Other Stories
Many Wise Fools & Other Stories
The Frog Prince & Other Stories
The Three Lemons & Other Stories
The Twelve-Headed Griffin & Other Stories
The Antelope Boy & Other Stories
Why the Fish Laughed & Other Stories
Two Cats & Other Stories
Three Stories
The Twilight of the Gods & Other Stories
The Son of Seven Queens & Other Stories
The Moon Maiden & Other Stories
The Metamorphosis & Other Stories
The Celestial Sisters & Other Stories
Tales from the Arabian Nights I
East of the Sun, West of the Moon & Other Stories
The Well at the End of the World & Other Stories

THE TWELVE-HEADED GRIFFIN
& OTHER STORIES

Edited & Introduced by

TAHIR SHAH

The Scheherazade Foundation

The Scheherazade Foundation CIC
85 Great Portland Street
London
W1W 7LT
United kingdom
www.SF.Charity
info@SF.Charity

First published by The Scheherazade Foundation CIC, 2023

THE TWELVE-HEADED GRIFFIN
&
OTHER STORIES

The Twelve-Headed Griffin
Roumanian Fairy Tales & Legends
E.B. Mawr
1881

The Tiger, the Brahman & the Jackal
Indian Fairy Tales
Joseph Jacobs
G. P. Putnam's Sons
1910

The Clever Deceiver
Aino Folk-Tales
Basil Hall Chamberlain
The Folk-Lore Society
1888

The Entangled Mermaid
Dutch Fairy Tales for Young Folks
William Elliot Griffis
Thomas Y. Crowell Co.
1918

The Golden Slipper
Cossack Fairy Tales & Folk Tales
George G. Harrap & Co.
1916

Jack & His Golden Snuff Box
English Fairy Tales
Joseph Jacobs
G. P. Putnam's Sons
1892

The Laughing Hippopotamus
American Fairy Tales
L. Frank Baum
George M. Hill Co.
1901

The Conceited Apple-branch
Fairy Tales of Hans Christian Andersen
Hans Christian Andersen
C. A. Reitzel
1843

The Seven Pigeons	The Talking Bird, the Singing Tree, &
Tales from the Lands of Nuts & Grapes	the Golden Water
Charles Sellers	*The Arabian Nights: Their Best-known*
Field & Tuer	*Tales*
1888	Charles Scribner's Sons
	1909

ISBN 978-1-915311-10-8

CONTENTS

Series Introduction

FROM EARLIEST CHILDHOOD, I was told stories.

Of course I was – most children are told stories.

After all, telling children stories is one of the foundations that makes their early experiences a childhood.

But as I think back to the first years of my own life, I find myself reeling from the sheer quantity of stories my infant ears took in.

Whereas other children my age were told stories for amusement, my parents (and the people they associated with) recounted the endless streams of tales for a different reason.

In their opinion, stories – and the ability to tell them – were part of an ancient alchemy... a way of processing complex ideas, of solving problems, and of developing the human mind.

My father, the writer and thinker Idries Shah, believed that folklore was the single most important breakthrough ever developed by the human species. The way he saw it, the rise of stories was as consequential as the development of the languages in which they were told.

He would say that, without stories and storytelling, humanity would never have evolved in the way that it

1

has – and that the folktales, which form a bedrock of ancient societies, are more precious than any physical artefact unearthed on an archaeological dig.

As the years of my own childhood slipped by, I found myself unbothered to work out the hidden layers within treasuries of stories – what my father called 'instruction manuals to the world'. Like everyone else, I simply absorbed the individual tales, delighting in them.

And that's it – the key point, the genius of stories and storytelling.

It's a thing I only grasped in adulthood… something that fascinates me deeply.

In the same way you can jump into a car and drive across the country without giving a second thought to the engine or how it works, you can appreciate stories without understanding the hidden layers and devices that make them what they are.

Stories are all around us.

They're in the TV and movies we so adore, in the video games we play, and of course in the books we read. They're in newspapers and magazines, too; in the conversations we share with old friends, and with new ones. They're on our mobile phones, in aeroplanes, in submarines, and even in our dreams.

Our obsession with, and craving for, stories rests squarely with the way we are so absorbed by them, just as it does with the way we don't need to continually consider how and why they work.

Throughout my life, I've devoted an increasing amount of time to gathering stories from all corners of the world.

It began in my late teens, when I began to criss-cross the continents in a crazed preoccupation with folklore. I developed a first-hand love affair with societies that, over millennia, gave birth to their own astonishing traditions of stories and storytelling.

Most of the time, when reading or listening to stories, we forget that these tales have been shaped through the passage of time. Like pebbles in a river smoothed by rushing waters, they were honed through centuries of telling and retelling.

When I was twelve years old, my father published a masterwork, *World Tales*. The first edition was very large and featured hundreds of original illustrations. The book was unlike any that had come before, for it detailed the provenance and history of each story told.

At bedtime one night, he presented me with an advanced copy. For as long as I could remember, my father had been talking about the project.

Having an actual copy in my hands at last was thrilling beyond words.

Peering down at me sternly, my father said:

'This is far more than a book, Tahir Jan. It's the foundation stone of a great building… a building that *is* human culture. As you grow older, and as you go out into the world, you will understand that the folklores contained between the covers of *World Tales* have brought amusement and educated, and have solved problems when they were needed most of all.'

My father was right.

When I eventually headed out into the wilds of the world for the first time, I discovered the stories contained in *World Tales* for myself, along with a great many more. Just as he said, the stories published in his treasury were the warp and weft threads of society. Stories are the matrix on which culture itself is based – a framework that enables daily life to continue as smoothly as it does.

In this series of books, we have drawn together stories from all over the world. It's a mission begun decades ago by *World Tales*.

Some of the pieces will be known to you, and others will not.

Some will be easy to comprehend, while others will be challenging, or even nonsensical.

I'd now like to note something else...

The Occidental world seems to assume stories must appear in certain regimented ways – presented with a well-defined beginning, a middle, and an end. You know what I mean: the protagonist winning against all odds, and the happy ending to it all.

In the ancient tradition of teaching stories, the kind recounted for an eternity around campfires in the desert and in longhouses deep in the jungle, there's no such standardisation.

Rather, there's usually a hotchpotch of conflicting threads: stories without a straight linear narrative but with an underlying turbulence that gets the reader, or the listener, to sit up and think.

At The Scheherazade Foundation, we are preoccupied with the way we can extract knowledge from stories – either deliberately, or in a less structured way.

We hold the firm opinion that, in order to remove the marrow from the bone stories are best served up in the way as they were passed from one generation to the next throughout human history.

In this series, we have drawn together tales that were gathered in particular during the nineteenth and early twentieth centuries. Spanning a vast range of cultures, they offer an extraordinary glimpse into the societies from which they are drawn – societies that were often changed shortly afterwards by social upheaval, technologies, and war.

Indeed, the fact any of them were recorded at all is a thing of wonder.

Intriguingly, some of the tales will now appear dated because vocabulary and writing styles have altered. But the fact that they seem old-fashioned is of great interest – proof of the way stories are constantly changing and evolving from one era to the next.

Over the last thirty years, I've gathered hundreds of tales on my own journeys, most of them spoken directly into my ears by storytellers and fellow travellers, by wizened old men in the middle of nowhere, and by anyone else good enough to indulge my pleas.

On all those zigzagging adventures, one story sticks out, tantalising me whenever I turn it around my head.

It was called 'The Man Who Turned into a Cat'.

The reason I mention it here is not because it was an especially fine tale, but rather because, from that moment, it affected the way I perceive the world.

It was as though I were a lock and that, by hearing the tale, a key had been slipped into me and turned.

Since first receiving it, I've never been quite the same, my state of consciousness having been flipped inside out.

The fellow traveller who recounted 'The Man Who Turned into a Cat' was lost in shadow, no more than a fragment of his left cheek protruding shyly into the light.

We were sitting on low divans in a teahouse in the ancient Afghan city of Herat.

When the tale had been whispered, I sat there in silence for a long while.

'What have you done to me?' I asked after a long pause.

The fellow traveller offered half a smile.

'*I* didn't do anything,' he replied. 'It's the story that's affected you – a story that I myself first heard when I was a child playing in the orchards of Balkh.'

Peering into the shadow, my eyes widened.

'I don't understand,' I said feebly. 'After all, it's not an especially grand story. There wasn't even a jinn.'

The traveller's mouth eased out from the shadows.

Very slowly, it grinned.

'Tales containing the greatest sustenance for a soul speak in the softest voice,' he said.

Tahir Shah

The Twelve-Headed Griffin

ONCE UPON A time there lived a king and queen whose greatest blessing from God was an only child of fifteen, named Theodor.

This boy from his childhood had learnt to ride, and to shoot with the bow, and had become a great proficient in both arts.

One day while practising archery, one of his arrows shot out of sight. The boy having marked the direction which it took, went to his father to request his swiftest horse, and money to go in search of his arrow.

His father gave him money, and permission to take the best horse in his stables.

With joy, the boy mounted swiftly and set off at a gallop.

After riding long and far, so far that the sun was disappearing from the horizon, he found himself in a vast prairie full of flowers. Stopping his horse, standing up in his stirrups, and shading his eyes with his hand, he perceived his arrow sticking in the ground. Dismounting he went quickly to the spot, seized the arrow with both hands, and with difficulty drew it out, leaving a great hole in the earth where it had penetrated. On looking down this hole, he

THE TWELVE-HEADED GRIFFIN & OTHER STORIES

saw at the bottom of it, a fine bull, and on the bull's back, a sword and a letter.

In great surprise at all these strange surroundings, he opened the letter and read,

'Whoever will take this bull and will give it three pecks of wheat and a gallon of wine, and continue to do so daily, the bull will have power to bring back to life the man who does this, no matter how many times he may die. This sword will turn into stone any living or inanimate object.'

Leading the bull, and strapping on the sword, the boy went on his way.

Towards night he reached a city and asked food and shelter of an old woman whom he met with. For himself a draught of water, for the bull a gallon of wine. The old woman fed him and his animals and gave the requisite wine to the bull. Water she said she had none, for in the whole city there was but one fountain, and that at the outskirts of the town; and that this fountain was guarded by a twelve-headed monster. Whoever needed water must sacrifice a young maiden to his appetite.

She told him that the next day it was the king's turn to give his daughter, and that this said king had made a proclamation to the effect that whoever would kill this monster and save his daughter, immense riches, and the hand of his daughter in marriage would be the reward.

The youth hearing all this, requested the old woman to awake him very early next morning, and to give him her water jars, saying he would fill them without giving anything to the monster. She promised this, and he soon fell into a sound sleep.

According to promise the next morning she aroused him, and taking his sword, his bow and arrows, and the water jars, set off for the well. Arriving there, he found the king's daughter weeping, and waiting to be eaten by the monster.

Said the youth to her, 'I have come to deliver you from the fangs of the monster, on one condition, that is, that you let me sit down by your side, lay my head on your lap, and if I should fall asleep, not to awake me until the monster shews himself.'

The young girl acquiesced with joy, and sitting clown beside her, the youth laid his head on her lap, and soon fell asleep. When the monster made his appearance, the girl was so overwhelmed with terror that she could not awake the youth but cried so plentifully that the scalding tears fell on his face. Jumping up, he saw the Monster before him. Charging his bow, he placed himself in front of the maiden; the monster seeing this, exclaimed,

'Stand aside, and let me take my right,' but the youth refused, it the same time drew the string of his bow and sent an arrow into the head which was stretched forth for his destruction.

The monster writhed with pain, and projected a second head, and then began a terrible strife. The youth's only defence was his courage and his bow, but the monster had his twelve heads, and his poisoned breath.

All that long summer's day they fought until evening; as night fell the boy could hardly stand from fatigue, had broken his bow, and had but one arrow in his quiver. But, on the other hand, the monster remained with only one head left out of the twelve.

At length, the youth took from the maiden's head, a long mesh of her rich hair – she, more dead than alive from terror – and with it bound his broken bow together, and the fight recommenced. Eventually the youth was victorious but fell down faint from loss of blood.

While both these young creatures lay fainting by the well side, there came up a slave, in the service of the king, to fetch water. Seeing the monster annihilated, he sought the young Princess, and finding that she was not dead, but only in a swoon, he threw water over her, and she quickly returned to her senses. The slave enquired of her who had killed the monster, and the maiden pointed to the apparently dead Theodor. Quick as thought the slave seized the youth's sword and cut his body into hundreds of pieces.

Then, collecting the twelve heads and tongues of the monster, and charging the maiden not to tell the king who had performed this mighty deed, he accompanied her to her father's palace.

Without the knowledge of the slave, the maid let fall a ring, and a handkerchief, beside the remains of the slaughtered youth.

When the king saw his daughter approach, he was overwhelmed with joy, and demanded the name of her deliverer.

'I, mighty king,' replied the slave, with pride.

'Can this be true?' enquired the king.

'It is true,' said his daughter, tremulously.

Though the king was sorely grieved that the deliverer of his child was a slave, yet he felt bound to fulfil the promise that she should be given him to wife.

While Theodor was lying hewed in morsels, by the side of the well, the old woman, his hostess, went to her stable to feed and give drink to the Bull. On seeing her, he refused all nourishment, telling her that 'he was thirsting after water, and not after wine, and that she must lead him to the public well; as now that the monster existed no longer, all the world could drink water in peace.' He bade her take with them a lump of salt, and soon they arrived at the well.

When the woman saw the morsels of what had once been the brave youth, she began to cry aloud; but the bull said to her,

'Don't distress yourself in that way but do as I tell you: take up piece by piece, limb by limb, and place them together, as they were in life.'

Obeying him, she put the different members once more together again. The bull licked well the lump of salt, then breathed over and licked the youth. Wherever his tongue passed over, the marks of the sword disappeared, and when he once more breathed into his face, Theodor opened his eyes and exclaimed: 'Have I slept long?'

'You would have slept longer,' said the woman, 'if your bull had not brought you to life.'

All was as a dream to him, and it was only after the bull had explained all that had occurred, that he understood why the maiden was no longer by his side.

On looking around him he saw the ring and the handkerchief which she had dropped; he took possession of them, and they returned to the old woman's dwelling.

The following day the king caused a proclamation to be issued to the effect that the nuptials of his beloved daughter, with Burcea, the slave, would take place in eight days. Burcea her deliverer, inviting the neighbouring kings and Nobles to come and do honour to the ceremony.

He sent for the court tailor, and commanded for his future son-in-law, clothing befitting his new rank. He ordered his treasurer to pay to Burcea any sum of money which he might demand.

On the appointed day, the guests were assembled in the Imperial Palace; but all were melancholy and angry that an ugly, uneducated slave should have gained such a high-born, lovely bride.

Amongst them all, the king was the most grieved, with the exception, perhaps, of his daughter, who reproached herself for not having told the truth to the king, her father. Burcea, the slave, alone, was joyful.

In those days, it was the custom at the marriage of a king's daughter, for each subject to offer a present, according to his means; so, Theodor begged the old woman to make him a cake, which she should take to the palace as his offering. She willingly agreed and began to make the cake. When it was ready for the oven, the youth slipped the ring into the middle of the cake and covered the paste over it.

The cake was baked, and wrapped in a clean napkin, and taken by the old woman to the gate of the palace. Her dress was so old and so patched, that the servants forbade her to enter; but the Princess looking from the window, gave orders that she should be admitted, and brought into her presence.

This was quickly done, and the cake was offered with humble wishes for her future happiness. The Princess took the cake and broke it; imagine her surprise when she found her ring in the middle of it!

'Where is the person who put this ring here?' asked she of the old woman.

'It must be the handsome boy that is at my cottage,' said she, 'he who was hewn to pieces by your slave, and was restored to life and health by his friendly bull.'

'Take this purse of money for yourself,' said the Princess,' and return quickly to your home, tell my deliverer to come here, for I am awaiting him.'

The woman sped swiftly on her errand. Full of joy, the youth seized his sword, and taking the handkerchief, set off for the Imperial palace.

On reaching the reception ball, he saw a crowd of Nobles, and in their centre, Burcea the slave, swelling with pride, and thinking himself as powerful as a Grand Vizier.

The youth passed speedily on, until he reached an apartment where the Princess was reclining. Seeing him, she sprang up, and flung herself into his arms, crying out, 'This is my deliverer; this is my deliverer.'

A crowd quickly surrounded them, and Theodor, in a clear voice, said: 'It is true that I am the deliverer of this maiden, who would have been eaten by the monster of the well. I killed him, and she was free; but faint from fatigue and loss of blood, when a slave of the king's, coming to the well, and seeing me in this state, hewed me to pieces with my own sword, and threatened the maiden with death, if she avowed the truth. At the same time, he possessed himself with the proofs of the monster's destruction. Had it not been for a bull, endowed with a miraculous power of bringing the dead to life, I should now be ready for my grave. Seeing that many wise men are here, and knowing that there is wisdom in numbers, I entreat all present to judge and condemn the one who is guilty.'

'To death! to death!' cried the crowd.

The Emperor, calling his servants, ordered them to bring two horses from his stables, one bred in the mountains, the other bred in the plains, and to tie the limbs of Burcea, the slave, to these two animals; his order was obeyed, the horses were let loose, and setting off in a gallop in different directions, the body of the slave was torn limb from limb.

And now, indeed, there was a real rejoicing; but the marriage, and the court festivities were all postponed, until the arrival of the parents of Theodor, who embraced him, and wept for joy and pride, that he had so nobly distinguished himself.

They built for him, and his young bride, a magnificent palace; at the entrance to the courtyard, there was also a well of purest water, apparently guarded and watched over by a gigantic bull in marble.

From: Roumanian Fairy Tales and Legends

The Tiger, the Brahman & the Jackal

ONCE UPON A time, a tiger was caught in a trap. He tried in vain to get out through the bars and rolled and bit with rage and grief when he failed.

By chance a poor Brahman came by.

'Let me out of this cage, oh pious one!' cried the tiger.

'Nay, my friend,' replied the Brahman mildly, 'you would probably eat me if I did.'

'Not at all!' swore the tiger with many oaths; 'on the contrary, I should be for ever grateful, and serve you as a slave!'

Now when the tiger sobbed and sighed and wept and swore, the pious Brahman's heart softened, and at last he consented to open the door of the cage. Out popped the tiger, and, seizing the poor man, cried, 'What a fool you are! What is to prevent my eating you now, for after being cooped up so long, I am just terribly hungry!'

In vain the Brahman pleaded for his life; the most he could gain was a promise to abide by the decision of the first three things he chose to question as to the justice of the tiger's action.

So, the Brahman first asked a pipal tree what it thought of the matter, but the pipal tree replied coldly, 'What have you to complain about? Don't I give shade and shelter to everyone who passes by, and don't they in return tear down my branches to feed their cattle? Don't whimper – be a man!'

Then the Brahman, sad at heart, went further afield till he saw a buffalo turning a well-wheel; but he fared no better from it, for it answered, 'You are a fool to expect gratitude! Look at me! Whilst I gave milk they fed me on cottonseed and oil-cake, but now I am dry they yoke me here, and give me refuse as fodder!'

The Brahman, still more sad, asked the road to give him its opinion.

'My dear sir,' said the road, 'how foolish you are to expect anything else! Here am I, useful to everybody, yet all, rich and poor, great and small, trample on me as they go past, giving me nothing but the ashes of their pipes and the husks of their grain!'

On this the Brahman turned back sorrowfully, and on the way, he met a jackal, who called out, 'Why, what's the matter, Mr. Brahman? You look as miserable as a fish out of water!'

The Brahman told him all that had occurred.

'How very confusing!' said the jackal, when the recital was ended; 'would you mind telling me over again, for everything has got so mixed up?'

The Brahman told it all over again, but the jackal shook his head in a distracted sort of way, and still could not understand.

'It's very odd,' said he, sadly, 'but it all seems to go in at one ear and out at the other! I will go to the place where it all happened, and then perhaps I shall be able to give a judgment.'

So, they returned to the cage, by which the tiger was waiting for the Brahman, and sharpening his teeth and claws.

'You've been away a long time!' growled the savage beast, 'but now let us begin our dinner.'

'Our dinner!' thought the wretched Brahman, as his knees knocked together with fright; 'what a remarkably delicate way of putting it!'

'Give me five minutes, my lord!' he pleaded, 'in order that I may explain matters to the jackal here, who is somewhat slow in his wits.'

The tiger consented, and the Brahman began the whole story over again, not missing a single detail, and spinning as long a yarn as possible.

'Oh, my poor brain! oh, my poor brain!' cried the jackal, wringing its paws.

'Let me see! how did it all begin? You were in the cage, and the tiger came walking by – '

'Pooh!' interrupted the tiger, 'what a fool you are! I was in the cage.'

'Of course!' cried the jackal, pretending to tremble with fright; 'yes! I was in the cage – no I wasn't – dear! dear! where are my wits? Let me see – the tiger was in the Brahman, and the cage came walking by – no, that's not it, either! Well, don't mind me, but begin your dinner, for I shall never understand!'

'Yes, you shall!' returned the tiger, in a rage at the jackal's stupidity; 'I'll make you understand! Look here – I am the tiger – '

'Yes, my lord!'

'And that is the Brahman – '

'Yes, my lord!'

'And that is the cage – '

'Yes, my lord!'

'And I was in the cage – do you understand?'

'Yes – no – Please, my lord – '

'Well?' cried the tiger impatiently.

'Please, my lord! – how did you get in?'

'How! – why in the usual way, of course!'

'Oh, dear me! – my head is beginning to whirl again! Please don't be angry, my lord, but what is the usual way?'

At this the tiger lost patience, and, jumping into the cage, cried, 'This way! Now do you understand how it was?'

'Perfectly!' grinned the jackal, as he dexterously shut the door, 'and if you will permit me to say so, I think matters will remain as they were!'

From: Indian Fairy Tales

The Clever Deceiver

A LONG, LONG time ago there was a rascal, who went to the mountains to fetch wood. As he did not know how to amuse himself, he climbed to the top of a very thick pine-tree. Having munched some rice, he stuck it about the branches of the tree, so as to make it look like birds' dung.

Then he went back to the village, to the house of the chief, and spoke thus to him: 'I have found a place where a beautiful peacock has its nest. Let us go there together! Being such a poor man, I feel myself unworthy of going too near the divine bird. You, being a rich man, should take the peacock. It will be a great treasure for you. Let us go!'

So, the chief went there with him. When the chief looked, there truly were many traces of birds' dung near the top of the tall pine-tree. He thought the peacock was there. So, he said:

'I do not know how to climb trees. Though you are a poor man you do know how to do so. So, go and get the peacock, and I will reward you well. Go and get the divine peacock!'

So, the poor man climbed the tree. When he was halfway up it, he said: 'Oh! sir, your house seems to be on fire.'

The chief was much frightened. Owing to his being frightened, he was about to run home.

19

Then the rascal spoke thus: 'By this time your house is quite burnt down. There is no use in your running there.'

The rich man thought he would go anywhere to die; so, he went towards the mountains. After he had gone a short way, he thought thus: 'You should go and see even the traces of your burnt house.'

So, he went down there. When he looked, he found that his house was not burnt at all. He was very angry and wanted to kill that rascal. Then the rascal came down.

The chief commanded his servants, saying: 'You fellows! This man is not only poor, but a very badly behaved deceiver. Put him into a mat and roll him up in it without killing him. Then throw him into the river. Do this!'

Thus spoke the chief.

The servants put the rascal into the mat and tied it round tight. Then two of them carried him between them on a pole to the riverbank. They went to the river.

The rascal spoke thus: 'Though I am a very bad man, I have some very precious treasures. Do you go and fetch them. If you do so, it can be arranged about their being given to you. Afterwards you can throw me into the river.'

Hearing this, the two servants went off to the rascal's house.

Meanwhile a blind old man came along from somewhere or other. His foot struck against something wrapped up in a mat. Astonished at this, he tapped it with his stick. Then the rascal said:

'Blind man! If you will do as I tell you, the gods will give you eyes, and you will be able to see. So do so. If you will untie me and do as I tell you, I will pray to the gods, and your eyes will be opened.'

The blind old man was very glad. He untied the mat and let the rascal out. Then the rascal saw that, though the man was old and blind, he was dressed very much like a god.

The rascal said: 'Take off your clothes and become naked, whereupon your eyes will quickly be opened.'

This being so, the blind old man took off his clothes. Then the rascal put him naked into the mat and tied it round tight. Then he went off with the clothes, and hid.

Shortly afterwards, the two men came, and said: 'You rascal! you are truly a deceiver. So, though you possess no treasures, you possess plenty of deceit. So now we shall fling you into the water.'

The blind old man said: 'I am a blind old man. I am not that rascal. Please do not kill me!'

But he was forthwith flung into the river. Afterwards the two men went home to their master's house.

Afterwards the rascal put on the blind old man's beautiful clothes. Then he went to the chief's house and said: 'My appearance of misbehaviour was not real. The goddess who lives in the river was very much in love with me. So, she wanted to take and marry my spirit after I should have been killed by being thrown into the river. So, my misdeeds are all her doing. Though I went to that goddess, I felt unworthy to become her husband, because I am a poor man. I have arranged so that you, who are the chief of the village, should go and have her, and I have come to tell you so. That being so, I am in these beautiful clothes because I come from the goddess.'

Thus, he spoke. As the chief of the village saw that the rascal was dressed in nothing but the best clothes, and thought that he was speaking the truth, he said: 'It will be well for me to be tied up in a mat and flung into the river.'

Therefore, this was done, just as had been done with the rascal, and he was drowned in the water.

After that, the rascal became the chief, and dwelt in the drowned chief's house. Thus, very bad men lived in ancient times also. So it is said.

From: Aino Folk-Tales

The Entangled Mermaid

LONG AGO, IN Dutch Fairy Land, there lived a young mermaid who was very proud of her good looks. She was one of a family of mere or lake folks dwelling not far from the sea. Her home was a great pool of water that was half salt and half fresh, for it lay around an island near the mouth of a river.

Part of the day, when the sea tides were out, she splashed and played, dived and swam in the soft water of the inland current. When the ocean heaved and the salt water rushed in, the mermaid floated and frolicked and paddled to her heart's content. Her father was a grey-bearded merryman and very proud of his handsome daughter. He owned an island near the river mouth, where the young mermaids held their picnics and parties and received the visits of young merrymen.

Her mother and two aunts were merwomen. All of these were sober folks and attended to the business which occupies all well brought up mermaids and merrymen. This was to keep their pool clean and nice. No frogs, toads or eels were allowed near, but in the work of daily housecleaning, the storks and the mermaids were great friends.

All water-creatures that were not thought to be polite and well behaved were expected to keep away. Even some silly birds, such as loons and plovers and all screaming and fighting creatures with wings, were warned off the premises, because they were not wanted. This family of merry folks liked to have a nice, quiet time by themselves, without any rude folks on legs, or with wings or fins from the outside. Indeed, they wished to make their pool a model, for all respectable mermaids and merrymen, for ten leagues around. It was very funny to see the old daddy merman, with a switch made of reeds, shooing off the saucy birds, such as the sandpipers and screeching gulls. For the bullfrogs, too big for the storks to swallow, and for impudent fishes, he had a whip made of seaweed.

Of course, all the mermaids in good society were welcome, but young mermen were allowed to call only once a month, during the week when the moon was full. Then the evenings were usually clear, so that when the party broke up, the mermen could see their way in the moonlight to swim home safely with their mermaid friends. For, there were sea monsters that loved to plague the merfolk and even threatened to eat them up! The mermaids, dear creatures, had to be escorted home, but they felt safe, for their mermen brothers and daddies were so fierce that, except sharks, even the larger fish, such as porpoises and dolphins were afraid to come near them.

One day daddy and the mother left to visit some relatives near the island of Urk. They were to be gone several days. Meanwhile, their daughter was to have a party, her aunts being the chaperones.

The mermaids usually held their picnics on an island in the midst of the pool. Here, they would sit and sun themselves. They talked about the fashions and the prettiest way to dress their hair. Each one had a pocket mirror, but where they kept these, while swimming, no mortal ever found out. They made wreaths of bright coloured seaweed, orange and black, blue, grey and red and wore them on their brows like coronets. Or they twined them, along with sea berries and bubble blossoms, among their tresses. Sometimes they made girdles of the strongest and knotted them around their waists.

Every once in a while, they chose a queen of beauty for their ruler. Then each of the others pretended to be a princess. Their games and sports often lasted all day, and they were very happy.

Swimming out in the salt water, the mermaids would go in quest of pearls, coral and other pretty things. These they would bring to their queen, or with them richly adorn themselves. Thus, the Mermaid Queen and her maidens made a court of beauty that was famed wherever mermaids and merrymen lived. They often talked about human maids.

'How funny it must be to wear clothes,' said one. 'Are they cold that they have to keep warm?'

It was a little chit of a mermaid, whose flippers had hardly begun to grow into hands, that asked this question.

'How can they swim with petticoats on?' asked another.

'My brother heard that real men wear wooden shoes! These must bother them, when on the water, to have their feet floating,' said a third, whose name was Silver Scales.

'What a pity they don't have flukes like us,' and then she looked at her own glistening scaly coat in admiration.

'I can hardly believe it,' said a mermaid, that was very proud of her fine figure and slender waist. 'Their girls can't be half as pretty as we are.'

'Well, I should like to be a real woman for a while, just to try it, and see how it feels to walk on legs,' said another, rather demurely, as if afraid the other mermaids might not like her remark.

They didn't. Out sounded a lusty chorus, 'No! No! Horrible! What an idea! Who wouldn't be a mermaid?'

'Why, I've heard,' cried one, 'that real women have to work, wash their husband's clothes, milk cows, dig potatoes, scrub floors and take care of calves. Who would be a woman? Not I' – and her snub nose – since it could not turn up – grew wide at the roots. She was sneering at the idea that a creature in petticoats could ever look lovelier than one in shining scales.

'Besides,' said she, 'think of their big noses, and I'm told, too, that girls have even to wear hairpins.'

At this – the very thought that anyone should have to bind up their tresses – there was a shock of disgust with some, while others clapped their hands, partly in envy and partly in glee.

But the funniest things the mermaids heard of were gloves, and they laughed heartily over such things as covers for the fingers. Just for fun, one of the little mermaids used to draw some bag-like seaweed over her hands, to see how such things looked.

One day, while sunning themselves in the grass on the island, one of their number found a bush on which foxgloves grew. Plucking these, she covered each one of her fingers with a red flower. Then, flopping over to the other girls, she held up her gloved hands. Half in fright and half in envy, they heard her story.

After listening, the party was about to break up, when suddenly a young merman splashed into view. The tide was running out and the stream low, so he had had hard work to get through the fresh water of the river and to the island. His eyes dropped salt water, as if he were crying. He looked tired, while puffing and blowing, and he could hardly get his breath. The queen of the mermaids asked him what he meant by coming among her maids at such an hour and in such condition.

At this the bashful merman began to blubber. Some of the mergirls put their hands over their mouths to hide their laughing, while they winked at each other, and their eyes showed how they enjoyed the fun. To have a merman among them, at that hour, in broad daylight, and crying, was too much for dignity.

'Boo-hoo, boo-hoo,' and the merman still wept saltwater tears, as he tried to catch his breath. At last, he talked sensibly. He warned the queen that a party of horrid men, in wooden shoes, with pickaxes, spades and pumps, were coming to drain the swamp and pump out the pool. He had heard that they would make the river a canal and build a dyke that should keep out the ocean.

'Alas! Alas!' cried one mermaid, wringing her hands. 'Where shall we go when our pool is destroyed? We can't live in the ocean all the time.' Then she wept copiously. The saltwater tears fell from her great round eyes in big drops.

'Hush!' cried the queen. 'I don't believe the merman's story. He only tells it to frighten us. It's just like him.'

In fact, the queen suspected that the merman's story was all a sham and that he had come among her maids with a set purpose to run off with Silver Scales. She was one of the prettiest mermaids in the company, but very young, vain and frivolous. It was no secret that she and the merman were in love and wanted to get married.

So, the queen, without even thanking him, dismissed the swimming messenger. After dinner, the company broke up and the queen retired to her cave to take a long nap! She was quite tired after entertaining so much company. Besides, since daddy and mother were away, and there were no beaus to entertain, since it was a dark night and no moon shining on the water, why need she get up early in the morning?

So, the Mermaid queen slept much longer than ever before. Indeed, it was not till near sunset the next day that she awoke. Then, taking her comb and mirror in hand, she started to swim and splash in the pool, in order to smooth out her tresses and get ready for supper.

But oh, what a change from the day before! What was the matter? All around her things looked different. The water had fallen low, and the pool was nearly empty. The river, instead of flowing, was as quiet as a pond. Horrors! When she swam forward, what should she see but a dyke and fences! An army of horrid men had come, when she was asleep, and built a dam. They had fenced round the swamp and were actually beginning to dig sluices to drain the land. Some were at work, building a windmill to help in pumping out the water.

The first thing she knew she had bumped her pretty nose against the dam. She thought at once of escaping over the logs and into the sea. When she tried to clamber over the top and get through the fence, her hair got so entangled between the bars that she had to throw away her comb and mirror and try to untangle her tresses. The more she tried, the worse became the tangle. Soon her long hair was all twisted up in the timber. In vain were her struggles to escape. She was ready to die with fright, when she saw four horrid men rush up to seize her. She attempted to waddle away, but her long hair held her to the post and rails. Her modesty was so dreadfully shocked that she fainted away.

When she came to herself, she found she was in a big, long tub. A crowd of curious little girls and boys were looking at her, for she was on show as a great curiosity. They were bound to see her and get their money's worth in looking, for they had paid a stiver (two cents) admission to the show. Again, before all these eyes, her modesty was so shocked that she gave one groan, flopped over, and died in the tub.

Woe to the poor father and mother at Urk! They came back to find their old home gone. Unable to get into it, they swam out to sea, never stopping till they reached Spitzbergen.

What became of the body of the Mermaid Queen?

Learned men came from Leyden to examine what was now only a specimen, and to see how mermaids were made up. Then her skin was stuffed, and glass eyes put in, where her shining orbs had been. After this, her body was stuffed and mounted in the museum, that is, set up above a glass case and resting upon iron rods. Artists came to Leyden to make pictures of her and no fewer than nine noblemen copied her pretty form and features into their coats of arms. Instead of the Mermaid's Pool is now a cheese farm of fifty cows, a fine house and barn, and a family of pink-cheeked, yellow-haired children who walk and play in wooden shoes.

So, this particular mermaid, all because of her entanglement in the fence, was more famous when stuffed than when living, while all her young friends and older relatives were forgotten.

From: Dutch Fairy Tales for Young Folks

The Golden Slipper

THERE WAS ONCE upon a time an old man and an old woman, and the old man had a daughter, and the old woman had a daughter. And the old woman said to the old man, 'Go and buy a heifer, that your daughter may have something to look after!'

So, the old man went to the fair and bought a heifer.

Now the old woman spoiled her own daughter but was always snapping at the old man's daughter. Yet the old man's daughter was a good, hard-working girl, while as for the old woman's daughter, she was but an idle girl. She did nothing but sit down all day with her hands in her lap.

One day the old woman said to the old man's daughter, 'Look now, you daughter of a dog, go and drive out the heifer to graze! Here you have two bundles of flax. See that you unravel it, and reel it, and bleach it, and bring it home all ready in the evening!'

Then the girl took the flax and drove the heifer out to graze.

So, the heifer began to graze, but the girl sat down and began to weep. And the heifer said to her, 'Tell me, dear little maiden, why do you weep?' –

'Alas! Why should I not weep? My stepmother has given me this flax and bidden me unravel it, and reel it, and bleach it, and bring it back as cloth in the evening.'

'Grieve not, maiden!' said the heifer, 'it will all turn out well. Lie down to sleep!'

So, she lay down to sleep, and when she awoke the flax was all unravelled and reeled and spun into fine cloth and bleached. Then she drove the heifer home and gave the cloth to her stepmother. The old woman took it and hid it away, that nobody might know that the old man's daughter had brought it to her.

The next day she said to her own daughter, 'Dear little daughter, drive the heifer out to graze, and here is a little piece of flax for thee, unravel it and reel it, or unravel it not and reel it not as you like best, but bring it home with you.'

Then she drove the heifer out to graze, and threw herself down in the grass, and slept the whole day, and did not even take the trouble to go and moisten the flax in the cooling stream. And in the evening, she drove the heifer back from the field and gave her mother the flax.

'Oh, mammy!' she said, 'my head ached so the whole day, and the sun scorched so, that I couldn't go down to the stream to moisten the flax.'

'Never mind,' said her mother, 'lie down and sleep; it will do for another day.'

And the next day she called the old man's daughter again, 'Get up, you daughter of a dog, and take the heifer out to graze. And here you have a bundle of raw flax; unravel it, heckle it, wind it on to your spindles, bleach it, weave with it, and make it into fine cloth for me by the evening!'

Then the girl drove out the heifer to graze. The heifer began grazing, but she sat down beneath a willow-tree, and threw her flax down beside her, and began weeping with all her might.

But the heifer came up to her and said, 'Tell me, little maiden, why do you weep?'

'Why should I not weep?' said she, and she told the heifer all about it.

'Grieve not!' said the heifer, 'it will all come right, but lie down to sleep.'

So, she lay down and immediately fell asleep. And by evening the bundle of raw flax was heckled and spun and reeled, and the cloth was woven and bleached, so that one could have made shirts of it straight off. Then she drove the heifer home and gave the cloth to her stepmother.

Then the old woman said to herself, 'How comes it that this daughter of the son of a dog has done all her task so easily? The heifer must have got it done for her; I know. But I'll put a stop to all this, you daughter of the son of a dog,' said she.

Then she went to the old man and said, 'Father, kill and cut to pieces this heifer of yours, for because of it your daughter does not a stroke of work. She drives the heifer out to graze and goes to sleep the whole day and does nothing.'

'Then I'll kill it!' said he.

But the old man's daughter heard what he said and went into the garden and began to weep bitterly.

The heifer came to her and said, 'Tell me, dear little maiden, why do you weep?'

'Why should I not weep,' she said, 'when they want to kill you?'

'Don't grieve,' said the heifer, 'it will all come right. When they have killed me, ask your stepmother to give you my entrails to wash, and in them you will find a grain of corn. Plant this grain of corn, and out of it will grow up a willow tree, and whatever you want, go to this willow tree and ask, and you shall have your heart's desire.'

Then her father slew the heifer, and she went to her stepmother and said, 'Prithee, let me have the entrails of the heifer to wash!'

And her stepmother answered, 'As if I would let anybody else do such work but you!'

Then she went and washed them, and sure enough she found the grain of corn, planted it by the porch, trod down the earth, and watered it a little. And the next morning, when she awoke, she saw that a willow tree had sprung out of this grain of corn, and beneath the willow tree was a spring of water, and no better water was to be found anywhere in the whole village. It was as cold and as clear as ice.

When Sunday came round, the old woman tricked her pet daughter out finely, and took her to church, but to the old man's daughter she said, 'Look to the fire, girl! Keep a good fire burning and get ready the dinner, and make everything in the house neat and tidy, and have your best frock on, and all the shirts washed against I come back from church. And if you have not all these things done, you shall say goodbye to dear life.'

So, the old woman and her daughter went to church, and the smart little stepdaughter made the fire burn up, and got the dinner ready, and then went to the willow tree and said, 'Willow tree, willow tree, come out of your bark! Lady Anna, come when I call you!'

Then the willow tree did its duty, and shook all its leaves, and a noble lady came forth from it. 'Dear little lady, sweet little lady, what are thy commands?' said she.

'Give me,' said she, 'a grand dress and let me have a carriage and horses, for I would go to God's House!'

And immediately she was dressed in silk and satin, with golden slippers on her feet, and the carriage came up and she went to church.

When she entered the church there was a great to-do, and everyone said, 'Oh! oh! oh! Who is it? Is it perchance some princess or some queen? For the like of it we have never seen before.'

Now the young Tsarevich chanced to be in church at that time. When he saw her, his heart began to beat stronger. He stood there and could not take his eyes off her. And all the great captains and courtiers marvelled at her and fell in love with her straightway. But who she was, they knew not. When service was over, she got up and drove away. When she got home, she took off all her fine things, and put on all her rags again, and sat in the window-corner and watched the folk coming from church.

Then her stepmother came back too. 'Is the dinner ready?' said she.

'Yes, it is ready.'

'Have you sewn the shirts?'

'Yes, the shirts are sewn too.'

Then they sat down to meat and began to relate how they had seen such a beautiful young lady at church.

'The Tsarevich,' said the old woman, 'instead of saying his prayers, was looking at her all the while, so goodly was she.'

Then she said to the old man's daughter, 'As for thee, girl! Though you have sewn the shirts and bleached them, you are but a dirty under-wench!'

On the following Sunday the stepmother again dressed up her daughter and took her to church. But, before she went, she said to the old man's daughter, 'See that you keep the fire in, girl!' and she gave her a lot of work to do.

The old man's daughter very soon did it all, and then she went to the willow tree and said, 'Bright spring willow, bright spring willow, change yourself, transform yourself!'

Then still statelier dames stepped forth from the willow tree, 'Dear little lady, sweet little lady, what commands have you to give?'

She told them what she wanted, and they gave her a gorgeous dress, and put golden shoes on her feet, and she went to church in a grand carriage. The Tsarevich was again there, and at the sight of her he stood as if rooted to the ground and couldn't take his eyes from her. Then the people began to whisper, 'Is there none here who knows her? Is there none who knows who such a handsome lady may be!'

And they began to ask each other, 'Do you know her? Do you know her?'

But the Tsarevich said, 'Whoever will tell me who this great lady is, to him will I give a sack-load of gold ducats!'

Then they inquired and inquired, and laid all their heads together, but nothing came of it. But the Tsarevich had a jester who was always with him, and used always to jest and cut capers whenever this child of the Tsar was sad. So now, too, he began to laugh at the young Tsarevich and say to him, 'I know how to find out who this fine lady is.'

'How?' asked the young Tsarevich.

'I'll tell you,' said the jester; 'smear with pitch the place in church where she is wont to stand. Then her slippers will stick to it, and she, in her hurry to get away, will never notice that she has left them behind her in church.'

So, the Tsarevich ordered his courtiers to smear the spot with pitch straightway. Next time, when the service was over, she got up as usual and hastened away, but left her golden slippers behind her. When she got home, she took off her costly raiment and put on her rags, and waited in the window-corner till they came from church.

When they came from church, they had all sorts of things to talk about, and how the young Tsarevich had fallen in love with the grand young lady, and how they were unable to tell him whence she came, or who she was, and the stepmother hated the old man's daughter all the more because she had done her work so nicely.

But the Tsarevich did nothing but pine away. And they proclaimed throughout the kingdom, 'Who has lost a pair of golden slippers?'

But none could tell. Then the Tsar sent his wise councillors throughout the kingdom to find her.

'If ye do not find her,' said he, 'it will be the death of my child, and then ye also are dead men.'

So, the Tsar's councillors went through all the towns and villages, and measured the feet of all the maidens against the golden slippers, and she was to be the bride of the Tsarevich whom the golden slippers fitted. They went to the houses of all the princes, and all the nobles, and all the rich merchants, but it was of no avail. The feet of all the maidens were either too little or too large. Then they hied them to the huts of the peasants.

They went on and on, they measured and measured, and at last they were so tired that they could scarce draw one foot after the other. Then they looked about them and saw a beautiful willow tree standing by a hut, and beneath the willow tree was a spring of water.

'Let us go and rest in the cool shade,' said they.

So, they went and rested, and the old woman came out of the hut to them.

'Hast thou a daughter, little mother?' said they.

'Yes, that I have,' said she.

'One or two?' they asked.

'Well, there is another,' said she, 'but she is not my daughter, she is a mere kitchen hand, the very look of her is nasty.'

'Very well,' said they, 'we will measure them with the golden slippers.'

'Good!' cried the old woman. Then she said to her own daughter, 'Go, my dear little daughter, tidy thyself up a bit, and wash thy little feet!'

But the old man's daughter she drove behind the stove, and the poor thing was neither washed nor dressed.

'Sit there, thou daughter of a dog!' said she.

Then the Tsar's councillors came into the hut to measure, and the old woman said to her daughter, 'Put out thy little foot, darling!'

The councillors then measured with the slippers, but they wouldn't fit her at all. Then they said, 'Tell us, little mother, where is thy other daughter?' –

'Oh, as for her, she is a mere girl, and besides she isn't dressed.'

'No matter,' said they; 'where is she?'

Then she came out from behind the stove, and her stepmother hustled her and said, 'Get along, hussy!'

Then they measured her with the slippers, and they fitted like gloves, whereupon the courtiers rejoiced exceedingly and praised the Lord.

'Well, little mother,' said they, 'we will take this daughter away with us.'

'What! Take a slattern like that? Why, all the people will laugh at you!'

'Maybe they will,' said they.

Then the old woman scolded and wouldn't let her go. 'How can such a girl become the consort of the Tsar's son?' screeched she.

'Nay, but she must come!' said they; 'go, dress thyself, maiden!'

'Wait but a moment,' said she, 'and I'll tire myself as is meet!'

Then she went to the spring beneath the willow tree, and washed and dressed herself, and she came back so lovely and splendid that the like of it can neither be thought of nor guessed at, but only told of in tales. As she entered the hut she shone like the sun, and her stepmother had not another word to say.

So, they put her in a carriage and drove off, and when the Tsarevich saw her, he could not contain himself.

'Make haste, O my father!' cried he, 'and give us thy blessing.'

So, the Tsar blessed them, and they were wedded. Then they made a great feast and invited all the world to it. And they lived happily together and ate wheat-bread to their hearts' content.

From: Cossack Fairy Tales & Folk Tales

Jack & His Golden Snuff Box

ONCE UPON A time, and a very good time it was, though it was neither in my time nor in your time nor in anyone else's time, there was an old man and an old woman, and they had one son, and they lived in a great forest. And their son never saw any other people in his life, but he knew that there was some more in the world besides his own father and mother, because he had lots of books, and he used to read every day about them. And when he read about some pretty young women, he used to go mad to see some of them; till one day, when his father was out cutting wood, he told his mother that he wished to go away to look for his living in some other country, and to see some other people besides them two.

And he said, 'I see nothing at all here but great trees around me; and if I stay here, maybe I shall go mad before I see anything.'

The young man's father was out all this time, when this talk was going on between him and his poor old mother.

The old woman began by saying to her son before leaving, 'Well, well, my poor boy, if you want to go, it's better for you to go, and God be with you.' – (The old woman thought for the best when she said that.) 'But stop a bit before you go.

Which would you like best for me to make you, a little cake and bless you, or a big cake and curse you?'

'Dear, dear!' said he, 'make me a big cake. Maybe I shall be hungry on the road.'

The old woman made the big cake, and she went on top of the house, and she cursed him as far as she could see him.

He presently met with his father, and the old man said to him: 'Where are you going, my poor boy?' when the son told the father the same tale as he told his mother.

'Well,' said his father, 'I'm sorry to see you going away, but if you've made your mind to go, it's better for you to go.'

The poor lad had not gone far, when his father called him back; then the old man drew out of his pocket a golden snuff box, and said to him: 'Here, take this little box, and put it in your pocket, and be sure not to open it till you are near your death.'

And away went poor Jack upon his road, and walked till he was tired and hungry, for he had eaten all his cake upon the road; and by this time night was upon him, so he could hardly see his way before him. He could see some light a long way before him, and he made up to it, and found the back door and knocked at it, till one of the maidservants came and asked him what he wanted. He said that night was on him, and he wanted to get some place to sleep. The maidservant called him in to the fire, and gave him plenty to eat, good meat and bread and beer; and as he was eating his food by the fire, there came the young lady to look at him, and she loved him well and he loved her. And the young lady ran to tell her father and said there was a pretty young man in the back kitchen; and immediately the gentleman came to him, and questioned him, and asked what work he could do. Jack said, the silly fellow, that he could do anything. (He meant that he could do any foolish bit of work that would be wanted about the house.)

'Well,' said the gentleman to him, 'if you can do anything, at eight o'clock in the morning I must have a great lake and some of-the largest man-of-war vessels sailing before my mansion, and one of the largest vessels must fire a royal salute, and the last round must break the leg of the bed where my young daughter is sleeping. And if you don't do that, you will have to forfeit your life.'

'All right,' said Jack; and away he went to his bed, and said his prayers quietly, and slept till it was near eight o'clock, and he had hardly any time to think what he was to do, till all of a sudden, he remembered about the little golden box that his father gave him.

And he said to himself: 'Well, well, I never was so near my death as I am now;' and then he felt in his pocket and drew the little box out.

And when he opened it, out there hopped three little red men, and asked Jack: 'What is your will with us?'

'Well,' said Jack, 'I want a great lake and some of the largest man-of-war vessels in the world before this mansion, and one of the largest vessels to fire a royal salute, and the last round to break one of the legs of the bed where this young lady is sleeping.'

'All right,' said the little men; 'go to sleep.'

Jack had hardly time to bring the words out of his mouth, to tell the little men what to do, but what it struck eight o'clock, when 'bang, bang' went one of the largest man-of-war vessels; and it made Jack jump out of bed to look through the window; and I can assure you it was a wonderful sight for him to see, after being so long with his father and mother living in a wood.

By this time Jack dressed himself, and said his prayers, and came down laughing; for he was proud, he was, because the thing was done so well.

The gentleman comes to him, and said to him: 'Well, my young man, I must say that you are very clever indeed. Come and have some breakfast.'

And the gentleman told him, 'Now there are two more things you have to do, and then you shall have my daughter in marriage.'

Jack got his breakfast, and had a good squint at the young lady, and she at him.

The other thing that the gentleman told him to do was to fell all the great trees for miles around by eight o'clock in the morning; and, to make my long story short, it was done, and it pleased the gentleman well.

The gentleman said to him: 'The other thing you have to do' – (and it was the last thing) – 'you must get me a great castle standing on twelve golden pillars; and there must come regiments of soldiers and go through their drill. At eight o'clock the commanding officer must say, "Shoulder up."'

'All right,' said Jack; when the third and last morning came the third great feat was finished, and he had the young daughter in marriage.

But, oh dear! There is worse to come yet.

The gentleman now made a large hunting party and invited all the gentlemen around the country to it, and to see the castle as well. And by this time Jack had a beautiful horse and a scarlet dress to go with them. On that morning his valet, when putting Jack's clothes by, after changing them to go a hunting, put his hand in one of Jack's waistcoat-pockets, and pulled out the little golden snuffbox, as poor Jack left behind in a mistake. And that man opened the little box, and there hopped the three little red men out, and asked him what he wanted with them.

'Well,' said the valet to them, 'I want this castle to be moved from this place far and far across the sea.'

'All right,' said the little red men to him; 'do you wish to go with it?'

'Yes,' said he.

'Well, get up,' said they to him; and away they went far and far over the great sea.

Now the grand hunting party comes back, and the castle upon the twelve golden pillars had disappeared, to the great disappointment of those gentlemen as did not see it before. That poor silly Jack is threatened by taking his beautiful young wife from him, for taking them in in the way he did. But the gentleman at last made an agreement with him, and he is to have twelve months and a day to look for it; and off he goes with a good horse and money in his pocket.

Now poor Jack went in search of his missing castle, over hills, dales, valleys, and mountains, through woolly woods and sheepwalks, further than I can tell you or ever intend to tell you. Until at last, he came up to the place where lives the king of all the little mice in the world. There was one of the little mice on sentry at the front gate going up to the palace, and did try to stop Jack from going in.

He asked the little mouse: 'Where does the king live? I should like to see him.'

This one sent another with him to show him the place; and when the king saw him, he called him in. And the king questioned him and asked him where he was going that way. Well, Jack told him all the truth, that he had lost the great castle, and was going to look for it, and he had a whole twelve months and a day to find it out.

And Jack asked him whether he knew anything about it; and the king said: 'No, but I am the king of all the little mice in the world, and I will call them all up in the morning, and maybe they have seen something of it.'

Then Jack got a good meal and bed, and in the morning he and the king went on to the fields; and the king called all the mice together and asked them whether they had seen the great beautiful castle standing on golden pillars. And all the little mice said, no, there was none of them had seen it.

The old king said to him that he had two other brothers: 'One is the king of all the frogs; and my other brother, who is the oldest, he is the king of all the birds in the world. And if you go there, maybe they know something about the missing castle.'

The king said to him: 'Leave your horse here with me till you come back, and take one of my best horses under you, and give this cake to my brother; he will know then who you got it from. Mind and tell him I am well and should like dearly to see him.'

And then the king and Jack shook hands together.

And when Jack was going through the gates, the little mouse asked him, should he go with him; and Jack said to him: 'No, I shall get myself into trouble with the king.'

And the little thing told him: 'It will be better for you to let me go with you; maybe I shall do some good to you some time without you knowing it.'

'Jump up, then.'

And the little mouse ran up the horse's leg, and made it dance; and Jack put the mouse in his pocket.

Now Jack, after wishing good morning to the king and pocketing the little mouse, which was on sentry, trudged on his way; and such a long way he had to go, and this was his first day. At last, he found the place; and there was one of the frogs on sentry, and gun upon his shoulder, and did try to hinder Jack from going in; but when Jack said to him that he wanted to see the king, he allowed him to pass; and Jack made up to the door. The king came out and asked him his business; and Jack told him all from beginning to end.

'Well, well, come in.'

He got good entertainment that night; and in the morning the king made such a funny sound and collected all the frogs in the world. And he asked them, did they know or see anything of a castle that stood upon twelve golden pillars; and they all made a curious sound, 'kro-kro, kro-kro', and said no.

Jack had to take another horse and a cake to this king's brother, who is the king of all the fowls of the air; and as Jack was going through the gates, the little frog that was on sentry asked John should he go with him. Jack refused him for a bit; but at last, he told him to jump up, and Jack put him in his other waistcoat pocket. And away he went again on his great long journey; it was three times as long this time as it was the first day; however, he found the place, and there was a fine bird on sentry. And Jack passed him, and he never said a word to him; and he talked with the king, and told him everything, all about the castle.

'Well,' said the king to him, 'you shall know in the morning from my birds whether they know anything or not.'

Jack put up his horse in the stable, and then went to bed, after having something to eat. And when he got up in the morning the king and he went on to some field, and there the king made some funny noise, and there came all the fowls that were in all the world.

And the king asked them; 'Did they see the fine castle?' and all the birds answered no.

'Well,' said the king, 'where is the great bird?'

They had to wait then for a long time for the eagle to make his appearance, when at last he came all in a perspiration, after sending two little birds high up in the sky to whistle on him to make all the haste he possibly could. The king asked the great bird, did he see the great castle? and the bird said: 'Yes, I came from there where it now is.'

'Well,' said the king to him; 'this young gentleman has lost it, and you must go with him back to it; but stop till you get a bit of something to eat first.'

They killed a thief and sent the best part of it to feed the eagle on his journey over the seas and had to carry Jack on his back. Now when they came in sight of the castle, they did not know what to do to get the little golden box.

Well, the little mouse said to them: 'Leave me down, and I will get the little box for you.'

So, the mouse stole into the castle, and got hold of the box; and when he was coming down the stairs, it fell down, and he was very near being caught. He came running out with it, laughing his best.

'Have you got it?' Jack said to him.

He said: 'Yes;' and off they went back again, and left the castle behind.

As they were all of them (Jack, mouse, frog, and eagle) passing over the great sea, they fell to quarrelling about which it was that got the little box, till down it slipped into the water. (It was by them looking at it and handing it from one hand to the other that they dropped the little box to the bottom of the sea.)

'Well, well,' said the frog, 'I knew that I would have to do something, so you had better let me go down in the water.'

And they let him go, and he was down for three days and three nights; and up he comes, and shows his nose and little mouth out of the water; and all of them asked him, did he get it? and he told them no.

'Well, what are you doing there, then?'

'Nothing at all,' he said, 'only I want my full breath;' and the poor little frog went down the second time, and he was down for a day and a night, and up he brings it.

And away they did go, after being there four days and nights; and after a long tug over seas and mountains, arrive at the palace of the old king, who is the master of all the birds in the world. And the king was very proud to see them and has a hearty welcome and a long conversation. Jack opened

49

the little box and told the little men to go back and to bring the castle here to them; 'and all of you make as much haste back again as you possibly can.'

The three little men went off; and when they came near the castle, they were afraid to go to it till the gentleman and lady and all the servants were gone out to some dance. And there was no one left behind there only the cook and another maid with her; and the little red men asked them which would they rather – go, or stop behind?

And they both said: 'I will go with you;' and the little men told them to run upstairs quick. They were no sooner up and in one of the drawing-rooms than here comes just in sight the gentleman and lady and all the servants; but it was too late. Off the castle went at full speed, with the women laughing at them through the window, while they made motions for them to stop, but all to no purpose.

They were nine days on their journey, in which they did try to keep the Sunday holy, when one of the little men turned to be the priest, the other the clerk, and third presided at the organ, and the women were the singers, for they had a grand chapel in the castle already. Very remarkable, there was a discord made in the music, and one of the little men ran up one of the organ-pipes to see where the bad sound came from, when he found out it only happened to be that the two women were laughing at the little red man stretching his little legs full length on the bass pipes, also his two arms the same time, with his little red night-cap, which he never forgot to wear, and what they never witnessed before, could not help calling forth some good merriment while on the face of the deep. And poor thing! Through them not going on with what they begun with, they very near came to danger, as the castle was once very near sinking in the middle of the sea.

At length, after a merry journey, they come again to Jack and the king. The king was quite struck with the sight of the castle; and going up the golden stairs, went to see the inside.

The king was very much pleased with the castle, but poor Jack's time of a twelvemonths and a day was drawing to a close; and he, wishing to go home to his young wife, gave orders to the three little men to get ready by the next morning at eight o'clock to be off to the next brother, and to stop there for one night; also to proceed from there to the last or the youngest brother, the master of all the mice in the world, in such place where the castle shall be left under his care until it's sent for. Jack takes a farewell of the king, and thanks him very much for his hospitality.

Away went Jack and his castle again and stopped one night in that place; and away they went again to the third place, and there left the castle under his care. As Jack had to leave the castle behind, he had to take to his own horse, which he left there when he first started.

Now poor Jack left his castle behind and faced towards home; and after having so much merriment with the three brothers every night, Jack became sleepy on horseback, and would have lost the road if it was not for the little men a-guiding him. At last, he arrived weary and tired, and they did not seem to receive him with any kindness whatever, because he had not found the stolen castle; and to make it worse, he was disappointed in not seeing his young and beautiful wife to come and meet him, through being hindered by her parents. But that did not stop long. Jack put full power on and despatched the little men off to bring the castle from there, and they soon got there.

Jack shook hands with the king and returned many thanks for his kingly kindness in minding the castle for him; and then Jack instructed the little men to spur up and put speed on. And off they went and were not long before they reached their journey's end, when out comes the young wife to meet him with a fine lump of a young son, and they all lived happy ever afterwards.

From: English Fairy Tales

The Laughing Hippopotamus

ON ONE OF the upper branches of the Congo River lived an ancient and aristocratic family of hippopotamuses, which boasted a pedigree dating back beyond the days of Noah – beyond the existence of mankind – far into the dim ages when the world was new.

They had always lived upon the banks of this same river, so that every curve and sweep of its waters, every pit and shallow of its bed, every rock and stump and wallow upon its bank was as familiar to them as their own mothers. And they are living there yet, I suppose.

Not long ago, the queen of this tribe of hippopotamuses had a child which she named Keo, because it was so fat and round. Still, that you may not be misled, I will say that in the hippopotamus language 'Keo', properly translated, means 'fat and lazy' instead of fat and round. However, no one called the queen's attention to this error, because her tusks were monstrous long and sharp, and she thought Keo the sweetest baby in the world.

He was, indeed, all right for a hippopotamus. He rolled and played in the soft mud of the riverbank, and waddled inland to nibble the leaves of the wild cabbage that grew there and was happy and contented from morning till night.

And he was the jolliest hippopotamus that ancient family had ever known. His little red eyes were forever twinkling with fun, and he laughed his merry laugh on all occasions, whether there was anything to laugh at or not.

Therefore, the people who dwelt in that region called him 'Ippi' – the jolly one, although they dared not come near. him on account of his fierce mother, and his equally fierce uncles and aunts and cousins, who lived in a vast colony upon the riverbank.

And while these people, who lived in little villages scattered among the trees, dared not openly attack the royal family of hippopotamuses, they were amazingly fond of eating hippopotamus meat whenever they could get it. This was no secret to the hippopotamuses. And, again, when the people managed to catch these animals alive, they had a trick of riding them through the jungles as if they were horses, thus reducing them to a condition of slavery.

Therefore, having these things in mind, whenever the tribe of hippopotamuses smelled the odour of the people, they were accustomed to charge upon them furiously, and if by chance they overtook one of the enemy they would rip him with their sharp tusks or stamp him into the earth with their huge feet.

It was continual warfare between the hippopotamuses and the people.

Gouie lived in one of the little villages. He was the son of the chief's brother and grandson of the village sorcerer, the latter being an aged man known as the 'the boneless wonder,' because he could twist himself into as many coils as a serpent and had no bones to hinder his bending his flesh into any position. This made him walk in a wabbly fashion, but the people had great respect for him.

Gouie's hut was made of branches of trees stuck together with mud, and his clothing consisted of a grass mat tied around his middle. But his relationship to the chief and the sorcerer gave him a certain dignity, and he was much addicted to solitary thought. Perhaps it was natural that these thoughts frequently turned upon his enemies, the hippopotamuses, and that he should consider many ways of capturing them.

Finally, he completed his plans, and set about digging a great pit in the ground, midway between two sharp curves of the river. When the pit was finished, he covered it over with small branches of trees, and strewed earth upon them, smoothing the surface so artfully that no one would suspect there was a big hole underneath. Then Gouie laughed softly to himself and went home to supper.

That evening the queen said to Keo, who was growing to be a fine child for his age: 'I wish you'd run across the bend and ask your Uncle Nikki to come here. I have found a strange plant and want him to tell me if it is good to eat.'

The jolly one laughed heartily as he started upon his errand, for he felt as important as a boy does when he is sent for the first time to the corner grocery to buy a yeast cake.

'Guk-uk-uk-uk! guk-uk-uk-uk!' was the way he laughed; and if you think a hippopotamus does not laugh this way you have but to listen to one and you will find I am right.

He crawled out of the mud where he was wallowing and tramped away through the bushes, and the last his mother heard as she lay half in and half out of the water was his musical 'guk-uk-uk-uk!' dying away in the distance.

Keo was in such a happy mood that he scarcely noticed where he stepped, so he was much surprised when, in the middle of a laugh, the ground gave way beneath him, and he fell to the bottom of Gouie's deep pit. He was not badly hurt, but had bumped his nose severely as he went down; so, he stopped laughing and began to think how he should get out again. Then he found the walls were higher than his head, and that he was a prisoner.

So, he laughed a little at his own misfortune, and the laughter soothed him to sleep, so that he snored all through the night until daylight came.

When Gouie peered over the edge of the pit next morning he exclaimed: 'Why, 'tis Ippi – the Jolly One!'

Keo recognized the scent of a man and tried to raise his head high enough to bite him. Seeing this, Gouie spoke in the hippopotamus language, which he had learned from his grandfather, the sorcerer. 'Have peace, little one; you are my captive.'

'Yes; I will have a piece of your leg, if I can reach it,' retorted Keo; and then he laughed at his own joke: 'Guk-uk-uk-uk!'

But Gouie, being a thoughtful man, went away without further talk, and did not return until the following morning. When he again leaned over the pit, Keo was so weak from hunger that he could hardly laugh at all.

'Do you give up?' asked Gouie, 'or do you still wish to fight?'

'What will happen if I give up?' inquired Keo.

The man scratched his woolly head in perplexity. 'It is hard to say, Ippi. You are too young to work, and if I kill you for food, I shall lose your tusks, which are not yet grown. Why, O Jolly One, did you fall into my hole? I wanted to catch your mother or one of your uncles.'

'Guk-uk-uk-uk!' laughed Keo. 'You must let me go, after all, for I am of no use to you!'

'That I will not do,' declared Gouie; 'unless,' he added, as an afterthought, 'you will make a bargain with me.'

'Let me hear about the bargain, for I am hungry,' said Keo.

'I will let you go if you swear by the tusks of your grandfather that you will return to me in a year and a day and become my prisoner again.'

The youthful hippopotamus paused to think, for he knew it was a solemn thing to swear by the tusks of his grandfather; but he was exceedingly hungry, and a year and a day seemed a long time off; so, he said, with another careless laugh:

'Very well; if you will now let me go, I swear by the tusks of my grandfather to return to you in a year and a day and become your prisoner.'

Gouie was much pleased, for he knew that in a year and a day Keo would be almost full grown. So, he began digging away one end of the pit and filling it up with the earth until he had made an incline which would allow the hippopotamus to climb out.

Keo was so pleased when he found himself upon the surface of the earth again that he indulged in a merry fit of laughter, after which he said: 'Good-by, Gouie; in a year and a day you will see me again.'

Then he waddled away toward the river to see his mother and get his breakfast, and Gouie returned to his village.

During the months that followed, as the man lay in his hut or hunted in the forest, he heard at times the faraway 'Guk-uk-uk-uk!' of the laughing hippopotamus. But he only smiled to himself and thought: 'A year and a day will soon pass away!'

Now when Keo returned to his mother safe and well, every member of his tribe was filled with joy, for the Jolly One was a general favourite. But when he told them that in a year and a day he must again become the slave of the man, they began to wail and weep, and so many were their tears that the river rose several inches.

Of course, Keo only laughed at their sorrow; but a great meeting of the tribe was called and the matter discussed seriously.

'Having sworn by the tusks of his grandfather,' said Uncle Nikki, 'he must keep his promise. But it is our duty to try in some way to rescue him from death or a life of slavery.'

To this all agreed, but no one could think of any method of saving Keo from his fate. So, months passed away, during which all the royal hippopotamuses were sad and gloomy except the Jolly One himself.

Finally, but a week of freedom remained to Keo, and his mother, the queen, became so nervous and worried that another meeting of the tribe was called. By this time the laughing hippopotamus had grown to enormous size and measured nearly fifteen feet long and six feet high, while his sharp tusks were whiter and harder than those of an elephant.

'Unless something is done to save my child,' said the mother, 'I shall die of grief.'

Then some of her relations began to make foolish suggestions; but presently Uncle Nep, a wise and very big hippopotamus, said: 'We must go to Glinkomok and implore his aid.'

Then all were silent, for it was a bold thing to face the mighty Glinkomok. But the mother's love was equal to any heroism.

'I will myself go to him, if Uncle Nep will accompany me,' she said, quickly.

Uncle Nep thoughtfully patted the soft mud with his fore foot and wagged his short tail leisurely from side to side.

'We have always been obedient to Glinkomok, and shown him great respect,' said he. 'Therefore I fear no danger in facing him. I will go with you.'

All the others snorted approval, being very glad they were not called upon to go themselves.

So, the queen and Uncle Nep, with Keo swimming between them, set out upon their journey. They swam up the river all that day and all the next, until they came at sundown to a high, rocky wall, beneath which was the cave where the mighty Glinkomok dwelt.

This fearful creature was part beast, part man, part fowl and part fish. It had lived since the world began. Through years of wisdom, it had become part sorcerer, part wizard, part magician and part fairy. Mankind knew it not, but the ancient beasts knew and feared it.

The three hippopotamuses paused before the cave, with their front feet upon the bank and their bodies in the water and called in chorus a greeting to Glinkomok. Instantly thereafter the mouth of the cave darkened, and the creature glided silently toward them.

The hippopotamuses were afraid to look upon it and bowed their heads between their legs.

'We come, O Glinkomok, to implore your mercy and friendly assistance!' began Uncle Nep; and then he told the story of Keo's capture, and how he had promised to return to the man.

'He must keep his promise,' said the creature, in a voice that sounded like a sigh.

The mother hippopotamus groaned aloud.

'But I will prepare him to overcome the man, and to regain his liberty,' continued Glinkomok.

Keo laughed.

'Lift your right paw,' commanded Glinkomok. Keo obeyed, and the creature touched it with its long, hairy tongue. Then it held four skinny hands over Keo's bowed head and mumbled some words in a language unknown to man or beast or fowl or fish.

After this it spoke again in hippopotamese: 'Your skin has now become so tough that no man can hurt you. Your strength is greater than that of ten elephants. Your foot is so swift that you can distance the wind. Your wit is sharper than the bulthorn. Let the man fear, but drive fear from your own breast forever; for of all your race you are the mightiest!'

Then the terrible Glinkomok leaned over, and Keo felt its fiery breath scorch him as it whispered some further instructions in his ear. The next moment it glided back into its cave, followed by the loud thanks of the three hippopotamuses, who slid into the water and immediately began their journey home.

The mother's heart was full of joy; Uncle Nep shivered once or twice as he remembered a glimpse he had caught of Glinkomok; but Keo was as jolly as possible, and, not content to swim with his dignified elders, he dived under their bodies, raced all around them and laughed merrily every inch of the way home.

Then all the tribe held high jinks and praised the mighty Glinkomok for befriending their queen's son. And when the day came for the Jolly One to give himself up to the man, they all kissed him goodbye without a single fear for his safety.

Keo went away in good spirits, and they could hear his laughing 'guk-uk-uk-uk!' long after he was lost in sight in the jungle.

Gouie had counted the days and knew when to expect Keo; but he was astonished at the monstrous size to which his captive had grown and congratulated himself on the wise bargain he had made. And Keo was so fat that Gouie determined to eat him – that is, all of him he possibly could, and the remainder of the carcass he would trade off to his fellow villagers.

So, he took a knife and tried to stick it into the hippopotamus, but the skin was so tough the knife was blunted against it. Then he tried other means; but Keo remained unhurt.

And now indeed the Jolly One laughed his most gleeful laugh, till all the forest echoed the 'guk-uk-uk-uk-uk!' And Gouie decided not to kill him, since that was impossible, but to use him for a beast of burden. He mounted upon Keo's back and commanded him to march. So Keo trotted briskly through the village, his little eyes twinkling with merriment.

The other people were delighted with Gouie's captive, and begged permission to ride upon the Jolly One's back. So Gouie bargained with them for bracelets and shell necklaces and little gold ornaments, until he had acquired quite a heap of trinkets. Then a dozen men climbed upon Keo's back to enjoy a ride, and the one nearest his nose cried out: 'Run, Mud-dog – run!'

And Keo ran. Swift as the wind he strode, away from the village, through the forest and straight up the riverbank. The men howled with fear; the Jolly One roared with laughter; and on, on, on they rushed!

Then before them, on the opposite side of the river, appeared the black mouth of Glinkomok's cave. Keo dashed into the water, dived to the bottom and left the people struggling to swim out. But Glinkomok had heard the laughter of Keo and knew what to do. When the Jolly One rose to the surface and blew the water from his throat there was no man to be seen.

Keo returned alone to the village, and Gouie asked, with surprise: 'Where are my brothers?'

'I do not know,' answered Keo. 'I took them far away, and they remained where I left them.'

Gouie would have asked more questions then, but another crowd of men impatiently waited to ride on the back of the laughing hippopotamus. So, they paid the price and climbed to their seats, after which the foremost said: 'Run, mud-wallower – run!'

And Keo ran as before and carried them to the mouth of Glinkomok's cave and returned alone.

But now Gouie became anxious to know the fate of his fellows, for he was the only man left in his village. So, he mounted the hippopotamus and cried: 'Run, river-hog – run!'

Keo laughed his jolly 'guk-uk-uk-uk!' and ran with the speed of the wind. But this time he made straight for the riverbank where his own tribe lived, and when he reached it he waded into the river, dived to the bottom and left Gouie floating in the middle of the stream.

The man began swimming toward the right bank, but there he saw Uncle Nep and half the royal tribe waiting to stamp him into the soft mud. So, he turned toward the left bank, and there stood the queen mother and Uncle Nikki, red-eyed and angry, waiting to tear him with their tusks.

Then Gouie uttered loud screams of terror, and, spying the Jolly One, who swam near him, he cried: 'Save me, Keo! Save me, and I will release you from slavery!'

'That is not enough,' laughed Keo.

'I will serve you all my life!' screamed Gouie; 'I will do everything you bid me!'

'Will you return to me in a year and a day and become my captive, if I allow you to escape?' asked Keo.

'I will! I will! I will!' cried Gouie.

'Swear it by the bones of your grandfather!' commanded Keo, remembering that men have no tusks to swear by.

And Gouie swore it by the bones of his grandfather.

Then Keo swam to Gouie, who clambered upon his back again. In this fashion they came to the bank, where Keo told his mother and all the tribe of the bargain he had made with Gouie, who was to return in a year and a day and become his slave.

Therefore, the man was permitted to depart in peace, and once more the Jolly One lived with his own people and was happy.

When a year and a day had passed Keo began watching for the return of Gouie; but he did not come, then or ever afterwards.

For the man had made a bundle of his bracelets and shell necklaces and little gold ornaments and had travelled many miles into another country, where the ancient and royal tribe of hippopotamuses was unknown. And he set up for a great chief, because of his riches, and people bowed down before him.

By day he was proud and swaggering. But at night he tumbled and tossed upon his bed and could not sleep. His conscience troubled him.

For he had sworn by the bones of his grandfather; and his grandfather had no bones.

From: American Fairy Tales

The Conceited Apple-branch

IT WAS THE month of May. The wind still blew cold; but from bush and tree, field and flower, came the welcome sound, 'Spring is come.' Wildflowers in profusion covered the hedges. Under the little apple tree, Spring seemed busy, and told his tale from one of the branches which hung fresh and blooming, and covered with delicate pink blossoms that were just ready to open.

The branch well knew how beautiful it was; this knowledge exists as much in the leaf as in the blood; I was therefore not surprised when a nobleman's carriage, in which sat the young countess, stopped in the road just by. She said that an apple branch was a most lovely object, and an emblem of spring in its most charming aspect.

Then the branch was broken off for her, and she held it in her delicate hand, and sheltered it with her silk parasol. Then they drove to the castle, in which were lofty halls and splendid drawing-rooms. Pure white curtains fluttered before the open windows, and beautiful flowers stood in shining, transparent vases; and in one of them, which looked as if it had been cut out of newly fallen snow, the apple-branch was placed, among some fresh, light twigs of beech.

It was a charming sight. Then the branch became proud, which was very much like human nature.

People of every description entered the room, and, according to their position in society, so dared they to express their admiration. Some few said nothing, others expressed too much, and the apple branch very soon got to understand that there was as much difference in the characters of human beings as in those of plants and flowers. Some are all for pomp and parade, others have a great deal to do to maintain their own importance, while the rest might be spared without much loss to society. So thought the apple branch, as he stood before the open window, from which he could see out over gardens and fields, where there were flowers and plants enough for him to think and reflect upon; some rich and beautiful, some poor and humble indeed.

'Poor, despised herbs,' said the apple branch; 'there is really a difference between them and such as I am. How unhappy they must be if they can feel as those in my position do! There is a difference indeed, and so there ought to be, or we should all be equals.'

And the apple branch looked with a sort of pity upon them, especially on a certain little flower that is found in fields and in ditches. No one bound these flowers together in a nosegay; they were too common; they were even known to grow between the paving-stones, shooting up everywhere, like bad weeds; and they bore the very ugly name of 'dog-flowers' or 'dandelions.'

'Poor, despised plants,' said the apple bough, 'it is not your fault that you are so ugly, and that you have such an ugly name; but it is with plants as with men, – there must be a difference.'

'A difference!' cried the sunbeam, as he kissed the blooming apple branch, and then kissed the yellow dandelion out in the fields. All were brothers, and the sunbeam kissed them– the poor flowers as well as the rich.

The apple bough had never thought of the boundless love of God, which extends over all the works of creation, over everything which lives, and moves, and has its being in Him; he had never thought of the good and beautiful which are so often hidden, but can never remain forgotten by Him – not only among the lower creation, but also among men. The sunbeam, the ray of light, knew better.

'You do not see very far, nor very clearly,' he said to the apple branch. 'Which is the despised plant you so specially pity?'

'The dandelion,' he replied. 'No one ever places it in a nosegay; it is often trodden under foot, there are so many of them; and when they run to seed, they have flowers like wool, which fly away in little pieces over the roads, and cling to the dresses of the people. They are only weeds; but of course, there must be weeds. O, I am really very thankful that I was not made like one of these flowers.'

There came presently across the fields a whole group of children, the youngest of whom was so small that it had to be carried by the others; and when he was seated on the grass, among the yellow flowers, he laughed aloud with joy, kicked out his little legs, rolled about, plucked the yellow flowers, and kissed them in childlike innocence.

The elder children broke off the flowers with long stems, bent the stalks one round the other, to form links, and made first a chain for the neck, then one to go across the shoulders, and hang down to the waist, and at last a wreath to wear round the head, so that they looked quite splendid in their garlands of green stems and golden flowers. But the eldest among them gathered carefully the faded flowers, on the stem of which was grouped together the seed, in the form of a white feathery coronal. These loose, airy wool-flowers are very beautiful, and look like fine snowy feathers or down. The children held them to their mouths and tried to blow away the whole coronal with one puff of the breath. They had been told by their grandmothers that whoever did so would be sure to have new clothes before the end of the year. The despised flower was by this raised to the position of a prophet or foreteller of events.

'Do you see,' said the sunbeam, 'do you see the beauty of these flowers? do you see their powers of giving pleasure?'

'Yes, to children,' said the apple bough.

By-and-by an old woman came into the field, and, with a blunt knife without a handle, began to dig round the roots of some of the dandelion plants, and pull them up. With some of these she intended to make tea for herself; but the rest she was going to sell to the chemist andobtain some money.

'But beauty is of higher value than all this,' said the apple tree branch; 'only the chosen ones can be admitted into the realms of the beautiful. There is a difference between plants, just as there is a difference between men.'

Then the sunbeam spoke of the boundless love of God, as seen in creation, and over all that lives, and of the equal distribution of His gifts, both in time and in eternity.

'That is your opinion,' said the apple-bough.

Then some people came into the room, and, among them, the young countess – the lady who had placed the apple bough in the transparent vase, so pleasantly beneath the rays of the sunlight. She carried in her hand something that seemed like a flower. The object was hidden by two or three great leaves, which covered it like a shield, so that no draught or gust of wind could injure it, and it was carried more carefully than the apple-branch had ever been.

Very cautiously the large leaves were removed, and there appeared the feathery seed-crown of the despised dandelion. This was what the lady had so carefully plucked, and carried home so safely covered, so that not one of the delicate feathery arrows of which its mist-like shape was so lightly formed, should flutter away. She now drew it forth quite uninjured, and wondered at its beautiful form, and airy lightness, and singular construction, so soon to be blown away by the wind.

'See,' she exclaimed, 'how wonderfully God has made this little flower. I will paint it with the apple branch together. Everyone admires the beauty of the apple bough; but this humble flower has been endowed by Heaven with another kind of loveliness; and although they differ in appearance, both are the children of the realms of beauty.'

Then the sunbeam kissed the lowly flower, and he kissed the blooming apple branch, upon whose leaves appeared a rosy blush.

From: Fairy Tales of Hans Christian Andersen

69

The Seven Pigeons

IN A DESERTED part of the rock-bound Cantabrian coast, a poor fisherman, named Pedro, discovered a lovely maiden, magnificently dressed, combing her long jet-black hair with a golden comb studded with diamonds.

It was still early morning, and the sun had not attained its greatest power; and as the tide was at its lowest, an innumerable number of ponds were formed by the rocks which, for a distance of half a mile, were left bare by the receding sea.

Seated near to one of these ponds, and cooling her feet in the water, sat this lovely maiden; and she was so intent on performing her toilet that she did not perceive Pedro, who, thinking she was a mermaid, and might therefore cast a spell over him, hid behind a ledge of rocks, and was able to see and hear her without being seen.

Pedro heard her singing the following words:

'I am daughter of a king
Who rules in Aragon,
My messengers they bring
Me food to live upon.
My father thinks me dead;
My death he did ordain,

70

For that I would not wed
A wicked knight of Spain.
But those whom he did send
To kill me in this place,
My youth they did befriend,
But cruel is my case.'

'Is it even so,' said Pedro to himself, 'that this lovely maiden is the daughter of a king? If I render her assistance I may incur great danger, and if I leave her to die it will be a crying shame; what, then, am I to do?'

As he was thus pondering in his mind, he heard a flapping of wings, and, looking in the direction whence the noise came, he saw a pair of perfectly white pigeons bearing a small basket between them, strung on a thin golden bar, which they held at each end between their beaks.

Descending, they deposited the basket by the side of the princess, who caressed them most tenderly, and then took from the basket some articles of food, which she greedily ate (for she had not eaten since the previous morning), and after having finished the contents, she again sang:

'I am daughter of a king,
Who thinks that I am dead;
Here on this beach I sing,
By pigeons I am fed.
Thank you, my pretty birds,
Who are so kind to me.
But what avail my words?
Oh, I a bird would be!'

This wish was no sooner uttered than Pedro, much to his astonishment, saw that the lovely princess had been turned into a white swan, with a small gold crown on the top of its head.

Expanding her wings, she gradually rose high above him, attended by the pigeons, and all three flew out to sea; when suddenly Pedro observed a magnificent ship not far from the coast, whose deck was of burnished gold, and her sides of ivory fastened with golden nails. The ropes were of thread of silver, and the sails of white silk, while the masts and yards were made of the finest sandalwood.

To the ship the three birds flew, and no sooner did they alight on the deck than Pedro observed that they were three beautiful maidens.

The princess sat on a richly ornamented chair, and the other two maidens on velvet cushions embroidered in gold at her feet.

Over them was spread a superb awning to shelter them from the rays of the sun, and the vessel glided about over the vast expanse of water, now in one direction, now in another, as if the breeze blew to suit the sails.

Pedro was so astonished at what he saw that at last, he got frightened, and, being young and nimble, he soon lost sight of the ship; but at every pace he seemed to hear a voice saying, 'Run not away, future king of Aragon!'

Pedro continued running till he left the beach far behind and was now in the pine forest; nor did he stop till he was in the densest part, when, for very fatigue, he threw himself on the ground, and then he distinctly heard a voice say, 'Pedro, you are destined to be king of Aragon; but tell no one.'

Not till then had he discovered that he was no longer dressed in fisherman's attire, but that his clothes were of the finest cloth fringed with gold lace.

Pedro, on seeing this, said, 'I am enchanted. That princess is indeed a mermaid and has cast a spell over me. I am undone, my eyes deceive me, and what I take for so much grandeur is but a deception.'

Saying which, he started to his feet, and hurried towards his village as fast as his legs would carry him.

Arrived at the fishing hamlet, all his old companions paid him such deference that he tried to get out of their way, thinking they did but laugh at him, and, arriving at the door of his widowed mother's cottage, he ran into the kitchen. His mother happened to be frying some fish, and when she saw a grand gentleman enter the apartment she took the pan off the fire, and, bowing low, said, 'My noble sir, this house is too humble for such as you; allow me to conduct you to his reverence's house, for there you will find accommodation more suited to your high estate.'

Pedro would have replied to his mother, and sought to kiss her hand and ask her blessing, after the custom of the country; but, on attempting to speak, his tongue hung out of his mouth, and he made so strange a noise and so gesticulated that his mother was glad to get out of the house, followed, however, by her son and a large crowd of villagers who had congregated to see the grand stranger.

As soon as it was known throughout the village of the arrival of the grand stranger the church bells pealed, and the parish priest mingled with the crowd desirous of seeing the new arrival; but as soon as Pedro commenced gesticulating as before, the priest and all the rest of the people were much frightened, for they thought that he was dangerously mad.

Pedro, noticing this, sorrowfully turned away from his native village and took the high road to the next town.

As he was going along, thinking of his present trouble, he observed a wide gate made of gold, opening into a beautiful garden, into which he hesitated not to enter; for he recollected what the wise woman of the village had once told him – that 'grand clothes beget respect.'

'Open wide those gates, O worker midst the flowers,' exclaimed Pedro to an old gardener (for he had now recovered his speech). 'I come in cloth of gold to speak unto my love.'

'Sir,' replied the old man, 'you may always enter here, for you are Don Pedro of Aragon, I well can see.'

'What very high balconies, a hundred feet in height!' exclaimed Pedro.

'Tell me, good old man, does the princess ever come there?'

'To those balconies so high, to feel the cooling breeze,' replied the gardener, 'the princess comes there every evening alone.'

'Should she ask you,' continued Pedro, 'who I am, tell her that I am your son come from a distant land, and I will help you to water the pinks.'

At her usual time the princess came to her favourite balcony, and seeing Pedro watering the flowers, she beckoned to him, saying: 'O waterer of the pinks, come a little nearer and speak to me.'

'Is it true that you desire to speak to me?' inquired Pedro of the princess.

'No mirror bright ever reflected the truth more correctly than the words I uttered conveyed my desire,' answered the princess.

'Here, then, you have me,' said Pedro. 'Order me as your slave; but give me, for I am thirsty, a small ewer of water.'

The princess poured some water into a silver goblet, and having handed it to Pedro, he exclaimed, 'And in this mirror bright of crystal water pure, which does reflect thy form, I quench my heart's deep thirst.'

'You see yonder palace at the end of the garden,' said the princess to Pedro. 'Well, in that palace you will be lodged for the night; but should you ever tell anyone what you see there, you will put yourself in danger and cause me great trouble.'

Pedro promised to keep secret whatever he might see that night, and bidding 'good night' to the princess, he hastened to the palace which the princess had pointed out to him, and, having entered it, he walked through the marble passage, which seemed to be interminable. On each side of him were rows of majestic columns, surmounted by gold capitals, and now and again he thought he saw the forms of lovely young maidens flitting among the columns.

Just as he was approaching a richly carved fountain surrounded by sacred palms, a maiden of surprising beauty seemed to be addressing a Moor in most impassioned tones, as if claiming his indulgence; but when Pedro got up to them, he discovered that both were the work of the statuary.

At every step the surroundings became more magnificent, and the carved ceiling was of such exquisite workmanship that it seemed rather the work of the loom, being so like the finest lace, than of the sculptor.

At last, he arrived at the end of this avenue of columns, and noticing a door in front of him, he opened it, and found himself standing on a marble quay, against which the sea waves were washing.

Scanning the vast expanse of water before him, he observed approaching him the same beautiful ship he had seen in the morning.

When the ship came alongside the quay, a sailor sprung on shore, and made her fast by a golden cable; then, addressing Pedro, he said, 'I am glad you have not kept us waiting, for our royal mistress is very wishful to consult you, as one of her favourite doves has broken its right wing, and if you cannot cure it, the princess will die of starvation.'

Pedro made no reply, but stepped on board the ship, which soon got under way, and within a short time they were approaching the coast he knew so well.

Having landed, Pedro saw the princess seated on the sand, nursing one of her white pigeons. 'Pedro of Aragon,' the princess exclaimed, 'a stranger dared to enter my royal father's garden, and in assisting to water the pinks he trod on the wing of my favourite pigeon, and he has broken it.'

'Señorita,' replied Pedro, 'the intruder did probably seek you, and had no idea of hurting the lovely bird.'

'That matters not,' continued the princess, 'for my principal supporter is wounded, and you must cure her. Cut out my heart, and steep this bird in my warm blood, and when I am dead, throw my body into the sea.'

'How can I kill one so lovely?' asked Pedro. 'I would rather die myself than hurt you!'

'Then you do not care for me, or else you would do as I bid you,' answered the princess.

'Princess, I cannot and will not kill you; but I will do anything else you bid me,' said Pedro.

'Well, then, since you will not kill me, I order you to take this pigeon back with you; for I know it was you who walked in my father's garden today,' continued the princess. 'And tomorrow evening, when you see that princess whom you saw today, you must kill her, and let her blood fall over this pretty bird.'

Pedro was now in great trouble, for he had promised the princess to do anything she told him to do, except killing her, and he could not break his word; so taking hold of the pigeon very gently, and bidding goodbye to the princess, he again stepped on board the ship, and so depressed was he that he had arrived at the marble quay without being aware of it.

On landing, he retraced his steps through the avenue of pillars, and found himself once more in the garden, where the old gardener was again watering the pinks.

'What very high balconies!' exclaimed Pedro. 'Tell me, old gardener of the ancient times, if the princess comes here today.'

'The princess loves the fresh sea breeze,' answered the old man, 'and tonight she will come to the balcony, for her noble lover will be waiting for her.'

'And who is the princess's lover?' inquired Pedro.

'If you will help me to water the pinks, I will tell you,' said the old man.

Pedro readily acquiesced and putting down the pigeon where he thought no harm would happen to it, he commenced assisting the gardener to water the pinks.

After a silence of a few minutes the gardener said, 'There were once seven pigeons who said, "Seven pigeons are we, and with other seven pigeons we might all be mated; but, as it is, we must remain seven pigeons."'

'Yes,' put in Pedro; 'but I want to know who the princess's lover is.'

The old man took no heed of the interruption, and continued: 'There were once seven pigeons who said, "Seven pigeons are we – "'

'Stop!' cried Pedro; 'I will have no such idle talk. Tell me who this noble lover is, or I will do you an injury.'

'Sir,' cried the gardener, with a very serious countenance, 'there were once seven pigeons who said, "Seven pigeons are we, and – "'

'Take your watering can,' shouted Pedro in disgust; 'I will not listen to your nonsense!'

'And yet there were once seven pigeons who said, "Seven pigeons are we;" and now the last of them is gone, for the noble lover has been false to his trust,' exclaimed the old man, looking very cunningly at Pedro.

At these words Pedro looked towards the place where he had placed the pigeon, and it was no longer there.

Seized with a fit of fury, he was about to lay hands on the gardener, when, to his astonishment, he found that he was also gone.

'I am undone,' cried the unhappy Pedro; 'and now I shall not see the princess again.'

Saying this, he fainted away, and might probably have remained there some time, but that he heard a voice saying, in a jocular manner: 'There were once seven pigeons who said, "Seven pigeons are we, and – " '

Pedro started to his feet, and close to him was standing the princess whom he had previously seen in the balcony.

'Why do you thus tease me, princess?' said Pedro. 'I want to hear no more about the seven horrid pigeons.'

'Don Pedro de Aragon,' answered the princess, 'I must tell you that the old gardener to whom you spoke is a magician, and he has possessed himself of the last means I had of regaining my liberty, for I am under his power. Is it not true that you came here with the purpose of killing me?'

'I was under a vow to do so,' replied Pedro; 'but I cannot kill you, although I would rather slay you, fair princess, than do you a more grievous injury.'

'Go back, then, to the unhappy lady whom you left on the seashore,and tell her that you have been false to your promises,' said the princess.

'How sorry I am,' exclaimed Pedro, 'that I was ever destined to be king of Aragon! When I was a poor fisherman, I was far happier than I am now!'

'Pedro of Aragon, the moon will be at the full tonight, and you may then rescue me,' said the princess, 'if you have the courage to meet the wicked magician in this garden at midnight, for then is his power weakest.'

'I am prepared for the worst,' replied Pedro, 'and I fear not your gaoler.'

'Well, then,' continued the princess, 'when the magician sees you, he will again tell you about the seven pigeons; but when he has finished, you must tell him that there were once seven wives who had only one husband, and that they are waiting outside to see him. Do as I tell you, and if you are not afraid of his anger, you may be able to free me.'

Pedro promised to do as he was told, and the princess having retired into the palace, Pedro amused himself by walking under the lofty balconies, watching the fireflies grow brighter as night came on.

Just about midnight the magician was seen watering the pinks, and as soon as he perceived Pedro he said: 'There were once seven pigeons who said, "Seven pigeons are we, and with other seven pigeons we might all be mated; but, as it is, we must remain seven pigeons."'

'Quite so,' put in Pedro. 'And once upon a time there were seven wives who had only one husband, and they are waiting outside to see him.'

The magician, at these words, lost all control over his temper; but Pedro heeded him not, rather did he endeavour to increase his rage by repeating all about the seven wives.

'I am undone!' cried the magician; 'but if you will induce the spirits of my seven wives to again seek the grave, I will give you what you want, and that is the princess.'

'Give me the princess first,' answered Pedro, 'and then I will free you of your wives.'

'Take her, then,' said the magician; 'here she is. And forget not what you have promised me, for I may tell you in confidence that a man with seven wives cannot play the magician.'

Pedro hurried away with the princess; and after they had been married and crowned, the princess, who was now queen, one day said to him: 'Pedro, the magician who held me captive from you was Rank, and therefore were the balconies so high. When you saw me on the beach fed by pigeons, it was that you should know my power; on the shore I was attended by winged messengers, and on the sea, I sailed about at pleasure.'

'But what about the wounded pigeon?' asked Pedro.

'Recollect, Pedro, what you said to me in the garden,' answered the princess – 'that you would rather slay me than do me a more grievous injury. That poor pigeon with its broken wing could no more hope to soar aloft than an injured woman to mix with her former associates.'

'And what about the seven wives who were waiting outside, and who so frightened the old magician, Rank?' continued Pedro.

'They are the seven deadly sins, who would each have a tongue for itself, and yet without tongues are enough to frighten Rank,' answered the princess.

'And who am I, then,' asked Pedro, 'to be so exalted now?'

'You are the wise man who strove to do his best, yet tried not to exalt himself above his position,' sweetly answered the princess.

'So that the magician Rank has unwillingly raised the poor fisherman to be king,' whispered Pedro.

'Not Rank alone, but much more so thy own worth.'

From: Tales from the Lands of Nuts and Grapes

The Talking Bird, the Singing Tree & the Golden Water

THERE WAS AN emperor of Persia named Kosrouschah, who, when he first came to his crown, in order to obtain a knowledge of affairs, took great pleasure in night excursions, attended by a trusty minister. He often walked in disguise through the city, and met with many adventures, one of the most remarkable of which happened to him upon his first ramble, which was not long after his accession to the throne of his father.

After the ceremonies of his father's funeral rites and his own inauguration were over, the new sultan, as well from inclination as from duty, went out one evening attended by his grand vizier, disguised like himself, to observe what was transacting in the city. As he was passing through a street in that part of the town inhabited only by the meaner sort, he heard some people talking very loud; and going close to the house whence the noise proceeded, and looking through a crack in the door, perceived a light, and three sisters sitting on a sofa, conversing together after supper.

By what the eldest said he presently understood the subject of their conversation was wishes: 'For,' said she, 'since we are talking about wishes, mine shall be to have the sultan's baker for my husband, for then I shall eat my fill of that bread, which by way of excellence is called the sultan's; let us see if your tastes are as good as mine.'

'For my part,' replied the second sister, 'I wish I was wife to the sultan's chief cook, for then I should eat of the most excellent dishes; and as I am persuaded that the sultan's bread is common in the palace, I should not want any of that; therefore, you see,' addressing herself to her eldest sister, 'that I have a better taste than you.'

The youngest sister, who was very beautiful, and had more charms and wit than the elder two, spoke in her turn: 'For my part, sisters,' said she, 'I shall not limit my desires to such trifles, but take a higher flight; and since we are upon wishing, I wish to be the emperor's queen-consort. I would make him father of a prince, whose hair should be gold on one side of his head, and silver on the other; when he cried, the tears from his eyes should be pearls; and when he smiled, his vermilion lips should look like a rosebud fresh-blown.'

The three sisters' wishes, particularly that of the youngest, seemed so singular to the sultan, that he resolved to gratify them in their desires; but without communicating his design to his grand vizier, he charged him only to take notice of the house, and bring the three sisters before him the following day.

The grand vizier, in executing the emperor's orders, would but just give the sisters time to dress themselves to appear before his majesty, without telling them the reason. He brought them to the palace, and presented them to the emperor, who said to them, 'Do you remember the wishes you expressed last night, when you were all in so pleasant a mood? Speak the truth; I must know what they were.'

At these unexpected words of the emperor, the three sisters were much confounded. They cast down their eyes and blushed, and the colour which rose in the cheeks of the youngest quite captivated the emperor's heart. Modesty, and fear lest they might have offended by their conversation, kept them silent.

The emperor, perceiving their confusion, said to encourage them, 'Fear nothing, I did not send for you to distress you; and since I see that without my intending it, this is the effect of the question I asked, as I know the wish of each, I will relieve you from your fears. You,' added he, 'who wished to be my wife, shall have your desire this day; and you,' continued he, addressing himself to the two elder sisters, 'shall also be married to my chief baker and cook.'

As soon as the sultan had declared his pleasure, the youngest sister, setting her elders an example, threw herself at the emperor's feet to express her gratitude. 'Sir,' said she, 'my wish, since it is come to your majesty's knowledge, was expressed only in the way of conversation and amusement. I am unworthy of the honour you do me and supplicate your pardon for my presumption.'

The other two sisters would have excused themselves also, but the emperor, interrupting them, said, 'No, no; it shall be as I have declared; the wishes of all shall be fulfilled.'

The nuptials were all celebrated that day, as the emperor had resolved, but in a different manner. The youngest sister's were solemnised with all the rejoicings usual at the marriages of the emperors of Persia; and those of the other two sisters according to the quality and distinction of their husbands; the one as the sultan's chief baker, and the other as head cook.

The two elder felt strongly the disproportion of their marriages to that of their younger sister. This consideration made them far from being content, though they were arrived at the utmost height of their late wishes, and much beyond their hopes. They gave themselves up to an excess of jealousy, which not only disturbed their joy, but was the cause of great trouble and affliction to the queen-consort, their younger sister. They had not an opportunity to communicate their thoughts to each other on the preference the emperor had given her but were altogether employed in preparing themselves for the celebration of their marriages.

Some days afterward, when they had an opportunity of seeing each other at the public baths, the eldest said to the other: 'Well, what say you to our sister's great fortune? Is not she a fine person to be a queen!'

'I must own,' said the other sister, 'I cannot conceive what charms the emperor could discover to be so bewitched by her. Was it a reason sufficient for him not to cast his eyes on you, because she was somewhat younger? You were as worthy of his throne, and in justice he ought to have preferred you.'

'Sister,' said the elder, 'I should not have regretted if his majesty had but pitched upon you; but that he should choose that little simpleton really grieves me. But I will revenge myself; and you, I think, are as much concerned as I; therefore, I propose that we should contrive measures and act in concert: communicate to me what you think the likeliest way to mortify her, while I, on my side, will inform you what my desire of revenge shall suggest to me.'

After this wicked agreement, the two sisters saw each other frequently, and consulted how they might disturb and interrupt the happiness of the queen. They proposed a great many ways, but in deliberating about the manner of executing them, found so many difficulties that they durst not attempt them. In the meantime, with a detestable dissimulation, they often went together to make her visits, and every time showed her all the marks of affection they could devise, to persuade her how overjoyed they were to have a sister raised to so high a fortune. The queen, on her part, constantly received them with all the demonstrations of esteem they could expect from so near a relative. Sometime after her marriage, the expected birth of an heir gave great joy to the queen and emperor, which was communicated to all the court, and spread throughout the empire. Upon this news the two sisters came to pay their compliments, and proffered their services, desiring her, if not provided with nurses, to accept of them.

The queen said to them most obligingly: 'Sisters, I should desire nothing more, if it were in my power to make the choice. I am, however, obliged to you for your goodwill, but must submit to what the emperor shall order on this occasion. Let your husbands employ their friends to make interest and get some courtier to ask this favour of his majesty, and if he speaks to me about it, be assured that I shall not only express the pleasure he does me but thank him for making choice of you.'

The two husbands applied themselves to some courtiers, their patrons, and begged of them to use their interest to procure their wives the honour they aspired to. Those patrons exerted themselves so much in their behalf that the emperor promised them to consider of the matter and was as good as his word; for in conversation with the queen he told her that he thought her sisters were the most proper persons to be about her but would not name them before he had asked her consent.

The queen, sensible of the deference the emperor so obligingly paid her, said to him, 'Sir, I was prepared to do as your majesty might please to command. But since you have been so kind as to think of my sisters, I thank you for the regard you have shown them for my sake, and therefore I shall not dissemble that I had rather have them than strangers.'

The emperor therefore named the queen's two sisters to be her attendants; and from that time, they went frequently to the palace, overjoyed at the opportunity they would have of executing the detestable wickedness they had meditated against the queen.

Shortly afterward a young prince, as bright as the day, was born to the queen; but neither his innocence nor beauty could move the cruel hearts of the merciless sisters. They wrapped him up carelessly in his cloths and put him into a basket, which they abandoned to the stream of a small canal that ran under the queen's apartment and declared that she had given birth to a puppy. This dreadful intelligence was announced to the emperor, who became so angry at the circumstance, that he was likely to have occasioned the queen's death, if his grand vizier had not represented to him that he could not, without injustice, make her answerable for the misfortune.

In the meantime, the basket in which the little prince was exposed was carried by the stream beyond a wall which bounded the prospect of the queen's apartment, and from thence floated with the current down the gardens. By chance the intendant of the emperor's gardens, one of the principal officers of the kingdom, was walking in the garden by the side of this canal, and, perceiving a basket floating, called to a gardener who was not far off to bring it to shore that he might see what it contained. The gardener, with a rake which he had in his hand, drew the basket to the side of the canal, took it up, and gave it to him. The intendant of the gardens was extremely surprised to see in the basket a child, which, though he knew it could be but just born, had very fine features. This officer had been married several years, but though he had always been desirous of having children, Heaven had never blessed him with any. This accident interrupted his walk: he made the gardener follow him with the child, and when he came to his own house, which was situated at the entrance to the gardens of the palace, went into his wife's apartment.

'Wife,' said he, 'as we have no children of our own, God has sent us one. I recommend him to you; provide him a nurse and take as much care of him as if he were our own son; for, from this moment, I acknowledge him as such.'

The intendant's wife received the child with great joy and took particular pleasure in the care of him. The intendant himself would not inquire too narrowly whence the infant came. He saw plainly it came not far off from the queen's apartment, but it was not his business to examine too closely into what had passed, nor to create disturbances in a place where peace was so necessary.

The following year another prince was born, on whom the unnatural sisters had no more compassion than on his brother but exposed him likewise in a basket and set him adrift in the canal, pretending, this time, that the sultana had given birth to a cat. It was happy also for this child that the intendant of the gardens was walking by the canal side, for he had it carried to his wife, and charged her to take as much care of it as of the former, which was as agreeable to her inclination as it was to his own.

The emperor of Persia was more enraged this time against the queen than before, and she had felt the effects of his anger if the grand vizier's remonstrances had not prevailed. The third year the queen gave birth to a princess, which innocent babe underwent the same fate as her brothers, for the two sisters, being determined not to desist from their detestable schemes till they had seen the queen cast off and humbled, claimed that a log of wood had been born and exposed this infant also on the canal. But the princess, as well as her brothers, was preserved from death by the compassion and charity of the intendant of the gardens.

Kosrouschah could no longer contain himself when he was informed of the new misfortune. He pronounced sentence of death upon the wretched queen and ordered the grand vizier to see it executed.

The grand vizier and the courtiers who were present cast themselves at the emperor's feet, to beg of him to revoke the sentence.

'Your majesty, I hope, will give me leave,' said the grand vizier, 'to represent to you, that the laws which condemn persons to death were made to punish crimes; the three extraordinary misfortunes of the queen are not crimes, for in what can she be said to have contributed toward them? Your majesty may abstain from seeing her – but let her live. The affliction in which she will spend the rest of her life, after the loss of your favour, will be a punishment sufficiently distressing.'

The emperor of Persia considered with himself, and, reflecting that it was unjust to condemn the queen to death for what had happened, said: 'Let her live, then; I will spare her life, but it shall be on this condition: that she shall desire to die more than once every day. Let a wooden shed be built for her at the gate of the principal mosque, with iron bars to the windows, and let her be put into it, in the coarsest habit; and every Muslim that shall go into the mosque to prayers shall heap scorn upon her. If anyone fail, I will have him exposed to the same punishment; and that I may be punctually obeyed, I charge you, vizier, to appoint persons to see this done.'

The emperor pronounced his sentence in such a tone that the grand vizier durst not further remonstrate; and it was executed, to the great satisfaction of the two envious sisters. A shed was built, and the queen, truly worthy of compassion, was put into it and exposed ignominiously to the contempt of the people, which usage she bore with a patient resignation that excited the compassion of those who were discriminating and judged of things better than the vulgar.

The two princes and the princess were, in the meantime, nursed and brought up by the intendant of the gardens and his wife with the tenderness of a father and mother; and as they advanced in age, they all showed marks of superior dignity, which discovered itself every day by a certain air which could only belong to exalted birth. All this increased the affections of the intendant and his wife, who called the eldest prince Bahman, and the second Perviz, both of them names of the most ancient emperors of Persia, and the princess, Periezade, which name also had been borne by several queens and princesses of the kingdom.

As soon as the two princes were old enough, the intendant provided proper masters to teach them to read and write; and the princess, their sister, who was often with them, showing a great desire to learn, the intendant, pleased with her quickness, employed the same master to teach her also. Her vivacity and piercing wit made her, in a little time, as great a proficient as her brothers. From that time, the brothers and sister had the same masters in geography, poetry, history, and even the secret sciences, and made so wonderful a progress that their tutors were amazed, and frankly owned that they could teach them nothing more. At the hours of recreation, the princess learned to sing and play upon all sorts of instruments; and when the princes were learning to ride she would not permit them to have that advantage over her, but went through all the exercises with them, learning to ride also, to bend the bow, and dart the reed or javelin, and oftentimes outdid them in the race and other contests of agility.

The intendant of the gardens was so overjoyed to find his adopted children so accomplished in all the perfections of body and mind, and that they so well requited the expense he had been at in their education, that he resolved to be at a still greater; for, as he had until then been content simply with his lodge at the entrance of the garden, and kept no country-house, he purchased a mansion at a short distance from the city, surrounded by a large tract of arable land, meadows, and woods. As the house was not sufficiently handsome nor convenient, he pulled it down, and spared no expense in building a more magnificent residence. He went every day to hasten, by his presence, the great number of workmen he employed, and as soon as there was an apartment ready to receive him, passed several days together there when his presence was not necessary at court; and by the same exertions, the interior was furnished in the richest manner, in consonance with the magnificence of the edifice. Afterward he made gardens, according to a plan drawn by himself. He took in a large extent of ground, which he walled around, and stocked with fallow deer, that the princes and princess might divert themselves with hunting when they chose.

When this country seat was finished and fit for habitation, the intendant of the gardens went and cast himself at the emperor's feet, and, after representing how long he had served, and the infirmities of age which he found growing upon him, begged that he might be permitted to resign his charge into his majesty's disposal and retire. The emperor gave him leave, with the more pleasure, because he was satisfied with his long services, both in his father's reign and his own, and when he granted it, asked what he should do to recompense him.

'Sir,' replied the intendant of the gardens, 'I have received so many obligations from your majesty and the late emperor, your father, of happy memory, that I desire no more than the honour of dying in your favour.'

He took his leave of the emperor and retired with the two princes and the princess to the country retreat he had built. His wife had been dead some years, and he himself had not lived above six months with his charges before he was surprised by so sudden a death that he had not time to give them the least account of the manner in which he had discovered them. The Princes Bahman and Perviz, and the Princess Periezade, who knew no other father than the intendant of the emperor's gardens, regretted and bewailed him as such, and paid all the honours in his funeral obsequies which love and filial gratitude required of them. Satisfied with the plentiful fortune he had left them, they lived together in perfect union, free from the ambition of distinguishing themselves at court, or aspiring to places of honour and dignity, which they might easily have obtained.

One day when the two princes were hunting, and the princess had remained at home, a religious old woman came to the gate, and desired leave to go in to say her prayers, it being then the hour. The servants asked the princess's permission, who ordered them to show her into the oratory, which the intendant of the emperor's gardens had taken care to fit up in his house, for want of a mosque in the neighbourhood. She bade them, also, after the good woman had finished her prayers, to show her the house and gardens and then bring her to the hall.

The old woman went into the oratory, said her prayers, and when she came out, two of the princess's women invited her to see the residence, which civility she accepted, followed them from one apartment to another, and observed, like a person who understood what belonged to furniture, the nice arrangement of everything. They conducted her also into the garden, the disposition of which she found so well planned, that she admired it, observing that the person who had formed it must have been an excellent master of his art. Afterward she was brought before the princess, who waited for her in the great hall, which in beauty and richness exceeded all that she had admired in the other apartments.

As soon as the princess saw the devout woman, she said to her: 'My good mother, come near and sit down by me. I am overjoyed at the happiness of having the opportunity of profiting for some moments by the example and conversation of such a person as you, who have taken the right way by dedicating yourself to the service of God. I wish everyone were as wise.'

The devout woman, instead of sitting on a sofa, would only sit upon the edge of one. The princess would not permit her to do so but rising from her seat and taking her by the hand, obliged her to come and sit by her.

The good woman, sensible of the civility, said: 'Madam, I ought not to have so much respect shown me; but since you command, and are mistress of your own house, I will obey you.'

When she had seated herself, before they entered into any conversation, one of the princess's women brought a low stand of mother-of-pearl and ebony, with a china dish full of cakes upon it, and many others set round it full of fruits in season, and wet and dry sweetmeats.

The princess took up one of the cakes, and presenting her with it, said: 'Eat, good mother, and make choice of what you like best; you had need to eat after coming so far.'

'Madam,' replied the good woman, 'I am not used to eat such delicacies, but will not refuse what God has sent me by so liberal a hand as yours.'

While the devout woman was eating, the princess ate a little too, to bear her company, and asked her many questions upon the exercise of devotion which she practised and how she lived; all of which she answered with great modesty. Talking of various things, at last the princess asked her what she thought of the house, and how she liked it.

'Madam,' answered the devout woman, 'I must certainly have very bad taste to disapprove anything in it, since it is beautiful, regular, and magnificently furnished with exactness and judgment, and all its ornaments adjusted in the best manner. Its situation is an agreeable spot, and no garden can be more delightful; but yet, if you will give me leave to speak my mind freely, I will take the liberty to tell you that this house would be incomparable if it had three things which are wanting to complete it.'

'My good mother,' replied the Princess Periezade, 'what are those? I entreat you to tell me what they are; I will spare nothing to get them.'

'Madam,' replied the devout woman, 'the first of these three things is the Talking Bird: so singular a creature that it draws around it all the songsters of the neighbourhood which come to accompany its voice. The second is the Singing Tree: the leaves of which are so many mouths which form a harmonious concert of different voices and never cease. The third is the Golden Water: a single drop of which being poured into a vessel properly prepared, it increases so as to fill it immediately, and rises up in the middle like a fountain, which continually plays, and yet the basin never overflows.'

'Ah! my good mother,' cried the princess, 'how much am I obliged to you for the knowledge of these curiosities! I never before heard there were such rarities in the world; but as I am persuaded that you know, I expect that you should do me the favour to inform me where they are to be found.'

'Madam,' replied the good woman, 'I should be unworthy the hospitality you have shown me if I should refuse to satisfy your curiosity on that point and am glad to have the honour to tell you that these curiosities are all to be met with in the same spot on the confines of this kingdom, toward India. The road lies before your house, and whoever you send needs but follow it for twenty days, and on the twentieth only let him ask the first person he meets where the Talking Bird, the Singing Tree and the Golden Water are, and he will be informed.'

After saying this, she rose from her seat, took her leave, and went her way.

The Princess Periezade's thoughts were so taken up with the Talking Bird, Singing Tree and Golden Water, that she never perceived the devout woman's departure, till she wanted to ask her some question for her better information; for she thought that what she had been told was not a sufficient reason for exposing herself by undertaking a long journey. However, she would not send after her visitor, but endeavoured to remember all the directions, and when she thought she had recollected every word, took real pleasure in thinking of the satisfaction she should have if she could get these curiosities into her possession; but the difficulties she apprehended and the fear of not succeeding made her very uneasy.

She was absorbed in these thoughts when her brothers returned from hunting, who, when they entered the great hall, instead of finding her lively and gay, as she was wont to be, were amazed to see her so pensive and hanging down her head as if something troubled her.

'Sister,' said Prince Bahman, 'what is become of all your mirth and gaiety? Are you not well? or has some misfortune befallen you? Tell us, that we may know how to act, and give you some relief. If anyone has affronted you, we will resent his insolence.'

The princess remained in the same posture some time without answering, but at last lifted up her eyes to look at her brothers, and then held them down again, telling them nothing disturbed her.

'Sister,' said Prince Bahman, 'you conceal the truth from us; there must be something of consequence. It is impossible we could observe so sudden a change if nothing was the matter with you. You would not have us satisfied with the evasive answer you have given; do not conceal anything, unless you would have us suspect that you renounce the strict union which has hitherto subsisted between us.'

The princess, who had not the smallest intention to offend her brothers, would not suffer them to entertain such a thought, but said: 'When I told you nothing disturbed me, I meant nothing that was of importance to you, but to me it is of some consequence; and since you press me to tell you by our strict union and friendship, which are so dear to me, I will. You think, and I always believed so too, that this house was so complete that nothing was wanting. But this day I have learned that it lacks three rarities which would render it so perfect that no country seat in the world could be compared with it. These three things are the Talking Bird, the Singing Tree, and the Golden Water.'

After she had informed them wherein consisted the excellency of these rarities, 'A devout woman,' added she, 'has made this discovery to me, told me the place where they are to be found, and the way thither. Perhaps you may imagine these things of little consequence; that without these additions our house will always be thought sufficiently elegant, and that we can do without them. You may think as you please, but I cannot help telling you that I am persuaded they are absolutely necessary, and I shall not be easy without them. Therefore, whether you value them or not, I desire you to consider what person you may think proper for me to send in search of the curiosities I have mentioned.'

'Sister,' replied Prince Bahman, 'nothing can concern you in which we have not an equal interest. It is enough that you desire these things to oblige us to take the same interest; but if you had not, we feel ourselves inclined of our own accord and for our own individual satisfaction. I am persuaded my brother is of the same opinion, and therefore we ought to undertake this conquest, for the importance and singularity of the undertaking deserve that name. I will take the charge upon myself; only tell me the place and the way to it, and I will defer my journey no longer than till tomorrow.'

'Brother,' said Prince Perviz, 'it is not proper that you, who are the head of our family, should be absent. I desire my sister should join with me to oblige you to abandon your design and allow me to undertake it. I hope to acquit myself as well as you, and it will be a more regular proceeding.'

'I am persuaded of your goodwill, brother,' replied Prince Bahman, 'and that you would succeed as well as myself in this journey; but I have resolved and will undertake it. You shall stay at home with our sister, and I need not recommend her to you.'

The next morning Bahman mounted his horse, and Perviz and the princess embraced and wished him a good journey. But in the midst of their adieus, the princess recollected what she had not thought of before.

'Brother,' said she, 'I had quite forgotten the accidents which attend travellers. Who knows whether I shall ever see you again? Alight, I beseech you, and give up this journey. I would rather be deprived of the sight and possession of the Talking Bird, the Singing Tree and the Golden Water, than run the risk of never seeing you more.'

'Sister,' replied Bahman, smiling at her sudden fears, 'my resolution is fixed. The accidents you speak of befall only those who are unfortunate; but there are more who are not so. However, as events are uncertain, and I may fail in this undertaking, all I can do is to leave you this knife.'

Bahman pulling a knife from his vestband, and presenting it to the princess in the sheath, said: 'Take this knife, sister, and give yourself the trouble sometimes to pull it out of the sheath; while you see it clean as it is now, it will be a sign that I am alive; but if you find it stained with blood, then you may believe me dead and indulge me with your prayers.'

The princess could obtain nothing more of Bahman. He bade adieu to her and Prince Perviz for the last time and rode away. When he got into the road, he never turned to the right hand nor to the left but went directly forward toward India. The twentieth day he perceived on the roadside a hideous old man, who sat under a tree near a thatched house, which was his retreat from the weather.

His eyebrows were as white as snow, as was also the hair of his head; his whiskers covered his mouth, and his beard and hair reached down to his feet. The nails of his hands and feet were grown to an extensive length, while a flat, broad umbrella covered his head. He had no clothes, but only a mat thrown round his body. This old man was a dervish for so many years retired from the world to give himself up entirely to the service of God that at last, he had become what we have described.

Prince Bahman, who had been all that morning very attentive to see if he could meet with anybody who could give him information of the place he was in search of, stopped when he came near the dervish, alighted, in conformity to the directions which the devout woman had given the

Princess Periezade, and leading his horse by the bridle, advanced toward him and saluting him, said: 'God prolong your days, good father, and grant you the accomplishment of your desires.'

The dervish returned the prince's salutation, but so unintelligibly that he could not understand one word he said. Prince Bahman, perceiving that this difficulty proceeded from the dervish's whiskers hanging over his mouth, and unwilling to go any further without the instructions he wanted, pulled out a pair of scissors he had about him, and having tied his horse to a branch of the tree, said: 'Good dervish, I want to have some talk with you, but your whiskers prevent my understanding what you say; and if you will consent, I will cut off some part of them and of your eyebrows, which disfigure you so much that you look more like a bear than a man.'

The dervish did not oppose the offer, and when the prince had cut off as much hair as he thought fit, he perceived that the dervish had a good complexion, and that he was not as old as he seemed.

'Good dervish,' said he, 'if I had a glass, I would show you how young you look: you are now a man, but before, nobody could tell what you were.'

The kind behaviour of Prince Bahman made the dervish smile and return his compliment. 'Sir,' said he, 'whoever you are, I am obliged by the good office you have performed and am ready to show my gratitude by doing anything in my power for you. You must have alighted here upon some account or other. Tell me what it is, and I will endeavour to serve you.'

'Good dervish,' replied Prince Bahman, 'I am in search of the Talking Bird, the Singing Tree and the Golden Water. I know these three rarities are not far from hence, but cannot tell exactly the place where they are to be found; if you know, I conjure you to show me the way, that I may not lose my labour after so long a journey.'

The prince, while he spoke, observed that the dervish changed countenance, held down his eyes, looked very serious, and remained silent, which obliged him to say to him again: 'Good father, tell me whether you know what I ask you, that I may not lose my time, but inform myself somewhere else.'

At last, the dervish broke silence. 'Sir,' said he to Prince Bahman, 'I know the way you ask of me; but the regard which I conceived for you the first moment I saw you, and which is grown stronger by the service you have done me, kept me in suspense as to whether I should give you the satisfaction you desire.'

'What motive can hinder you?' replied the prince; 'and what difficulties do you find in so doing?'

'I will tell you,' replied the dervish; 'the danger to which you are going to expose yourself is greater than you may suppose. A number of gentlemen of as much bravery as you can possibly possess have passed this way and asked me the same question. When I had used all my endeavours to persuade them to desist, they would not believe me; at last, I yielded to their importunities. I was compelled to show them the way, and I can assure you they have all perished, for I have not seen one come back. Therefore, if you have any regard for your life, take my advice, go no farther, but return home.'

Prince Bahman persisted in his resolution.

'I will not suppose,' said he to the dervish, 'but that your advice is sincere. I am obliged to you for the friendship you express for me; but whatever may be the danger, nothing shall make me change my intention: whoever attacks me, I am well armed, and can say I am as brave as anyone.'

'But they who will attack you are not to be seen,' replied the dervish; 'how will you defend yourself against invisible persons?'

'It is no matter,' answered the prince, 'all you say shall not persuade me to do anything contrary to my duty. Since you know the way, I conjure you once more to inform me.'

When the dervish found he could not prevail upon Prince Bahman, and that he was obstinately bent to pursue his journey, notwithstanding his friendly remonstrance, he put his hand into a bag that lay by him and pulled out a bowl, which he presented to him.

'Since I cannot prevail on you to attend to my advice,' said he, 'take this bowl and when you are on horseback throw it before you, and follow it to the foot of a mountain, where it will stop. As soon as the bowl stops, alight, leave your horse with the bridle over his neck, and he will stand in the same place till you return. As you ascend, you will see on your right and left a great number of large black stones and will hear on all sides a confusion of voices, which will utter a thousand abuses to discourage you, and prevent your reaching the summit of the mountain. Be not afraid; but, above all things, do not turn your head to look behind you, for in that instant you will be changed into such a black stone as those you see, which are all youths who have failed in this enterprise. If you escape the danger of which I give you but a faint idea, and get to the top of the mountain, you will see a cage, and in that cage is the bird you seek; ask him which are the Singing Tree and the Golden Water, and he will tell you. I have nothing more to say; this is what you have to do, and if you are prudent, you will take my advice and not expose your life. Consider once more while you have time that the difficulties are almost insuperable.'

'I am obliged to you for your advice,' replied Prince Bahman, after he had received the bowl, 'but cannot follow it. However, I will endeavour to conform myself to that part of it which bids me not to look behind me, and I hope to come and thank you when I have obtained what I am seeking.'

After these words, to which the dervish made no other answer than that he should be overjoyed to see him again, the prince mounted his horse, took leave of the dervish with a respectful salute, and threw the bowl before him.

The bowl rolled away with as much swiftness as when Prince Bahman first hurled it from his hand, which obliged him to put his horse to the same pace to avoid losing sight of it, and when it had reached the foot of the mountain, it stopped. The prince alighted from his horse, laid the bridle on his neck, and having first surveyed the mountain and seen the black stones, began to ascend, but had not gone four steps before he heard the voices mentioned by the dervish, though he could see nobody.

Some said: 'Where is that fool going? Where is he going? What would he have? Do not let him pass.'

Others: 'Stop him, catch him, kill him'.

And others with a voice like thunder: 'Thief! assassin! murderer!'

While some in a gibing tone cried: 'No, no, do not hurt him; let the pretty fellow pass, the cage and bird are kept for him.'

Notwithstanding all these troublesome voices, Prince Bahman ascended with resolution for some time, but the voices redoubled with so loud a din, both behind and before, that at last, he was seized with dread, his legs trembled under him and he staggered. And finding that his strength failed him, he forgot the dervish's advice, turned about to run down the hill, and was that instant changed into a black stone; a metamorphosis which had happened to many before him who had attempted the ascent. His horse, likewise, underwent the same change.

From the time of Prince Bahman's departure, the Princess Periezade always wore the knife and sheath in her girdle, and pulled it out several times in a day, to know whether her brother was alive. She had the consolation to understand he was in perfect health and to talk of him frequently with Prince Perviz. On the fatal day that Prince Bahman was transformed into a stone, as Prince Perviz and the princess were talking together in the evening, as usual, the prince desired his sister to pull out the knife to know how their brother did. The princess readily complied, and seeing the blood run down the point was seized with so much horror that she threw it down.

'Ah! my dear brother,' cried she, 'I have been the cause of your death, and shall never see you more! Why did I tell you of the Talking Bird, Singing Tree and Golden Water; or rather, of what importance was it to me to know whether the devout woman thought this house ugly or handsome, or complete or not? I wish to Heaven she had never addressed herself to me!'

Prince Perviz was as much afflicted at the death of Prince Bahman as the princess, but not to waste time in needless regret, as he knew that she still passionately desired possession of the marvellous treasures, he interrupted her, saying: 'Sister, our regret for our brother is vain; our lamentations cannot restore him to life; it is the will of God; we must submit and adore the decrees of the Almighty without searching into them. Why should you now doubt of the truth of what the holy woman told you? Do you think she spoke to you of three things that were not in being, and that she invented them to deceive you who had received her with so much goodness and civility? Let us rather believe that our brother's death is owing to some error on his part, or some accident which we cannot conceive. It ought not therefore to prevent us from pursuing our object. I offered to go this journey and am now more resolved than ever; his example has no effect upon my resolution; tomorrow I will depart.'

The princess did all she could to dissuade Prince Perviz, conjuring him not to expose her to the danger of losing two brothers; but he was obstinate, and all the remonstrances she could urge had no effect upon him. Before he went, that she might know what success he had, he left her a string of a hundred pearls, telling her that if they would not run when she should count them upon the string, but remain fixed, that would be a certain sign he had undergone the same fate as his brother; but at the same time told her he hoped it would never happen, but that he should have the delight of seeing her again.

Prince Perviz, on the twentieth day after his departure, met the same dervish in the same place as his brother Bahman had done before him. He went directly up to him, and after he had saluted, asked him if he could tell him where to find the Talking Bird, the Singing Tree and the Golden Water. The dervish urged the same remonstrances as he had done to Prince Bahman, telling him that a young gentleman, who very much resembled him, was with him a short time before. That, overcome by his importunity, he had shown him the way, given him a guide, and told him how he should act to succeed, but that he had not seen him since, and doubted not but he had shared the same fate as all other adventurers.

'Good dervish,' answered Prince Perviz, 'I know whom you speak of; he was my elder brother, and I am informed of the certainty of his death but know not the cause.'

'I can tell you,' replied the dervish; 'he was changed into a black stone, as all I speak of have been; and you must expect the same transformation, unless you observe more exactly than he has done the advice I gave him, in case you persist in your resolution, which I once more entreat you to renounce.'

'Dervish,' said Prince Perviz, 'I cannot sufficiently express how much I am obliged for the concern you take in my life, who am a stranger to you, and have done nothing to deserve your kindness; but I thoroughly considered this enterprise before I undertook it; therefore, I beg of you to do me the same favour you have done my brother. Perhaps I may have better success in following your directions.'

'Since I cannot prevail with you,' said the dervish, 'to give up your obstinate resolution, if my age did not prevent me, and I could stand, I would get up to reach you a bowl I have here, which will show you the way.'

Without giving the dervish time to say more, the prince alighted from his horse and went to the dervish, who had taken a bowl out of his bag, in which he had a great many, and gave it him, with the same directions he had given Prince Bahman; and after warning him not to be discouraged by the voices he should hear, however threatening they might be, but to continue his way up the hill till he saw the cage and bird, he let him depart.

Prince Perviz thanked the dervish, and when he had remounted and taken leave, threw the bowl before his horse, and spurring him at the same time, followed it. When the bowl came to the bottom of the hill it stopped, the prince alighted, and stood some time to recollect the dervish's directions. He encouraged himself and began to walk up with a resolution to reach the summit.

But before he had gone above six steps, he heard a voice, which seemed to be near, as of a man behind him, say in an insulting tone: 'Stay, rash youth, that I may punish you for your presumption.'

Upon this affront the prince, forgetting the dervish's advice, clapped his hand upon his sword, drew it, and turned about to revenge himself; but had scarcely time to see that nobody followed him before he and his horse were changed into black stones.

In the meantime, the Princess Periezade, several times a day after her brother's departure, counted her chaplet. She did not omit it at night, but when she went to bed put it about her neck, and in the morning when she awoke counted over the pearls again to see if they would slide.

The day that Prince Perviz was transformed into a stone she was counting over the pearls as she used to do, when all at once they became immovably fixed, a certain token that the prince, her brother, was dead. As she had determined what to do in case it should so happen, she lost no time in outward demonstrations of grief, which she concealed as much as possible, but having disguised herself in man's apparel, she mounted her horse the next morning, armed and equipped, having told her servants she should return in two or three days, and took the same road that her brothers had done.

The princess, who had been used to ride on horseback in hunting, supported the fatigue of so long a journey better than most ladies could have done; and as she made the same stages as her brothers, she also met with the dervish on the twentieth day. When she came near him, she alighted from her horse, leading him by the bridle, went and sat down by the dervish, and after she had saluted him, said: 'Good dervish, give me leave to rest myself; and do me the favour to tell me if you have not heard that there are somewhere in this neighbourhood a Talking Bird, a Singing Tree and Golden Water.'

'Princess,' answered the dervish, 'for so I must call you, since by your voice I know you to be a woman disguised in man's apparel, I know the place well where these things are to be found; but what makes you ask me this question?'

'Good dervish,' replied the princess, 'I have had such a flattering relation of them given me, that I have a great desire to possess them.'

'Madam,' replied the dervish, 'you have been told the truth. These curiosities are more singular than they have been represented, but you have not been made acquainted with the difficulties which must be surmounted in order to obtain them. If you had been fully informed of these, you would not have undertaken so dangerous an enterprise. Take my advice, return and do not urge me to contribute toward your ruin.'

'Good father,' said the princess, 'I have travelled a great way, and should be sorry to return without executing my design. You talk of difficulties and danger of life, but you do not tell me what those difficulties are, and wherein the danger consists. This is what I desire to know, that I may consider and judge whether I can trust my courage and strength to brave them.'

The dervish repeated to the princess what he had said to the Princes Bahman and Perviz, exaggerating the difficulties of climbing up to the top of the mountain, where she was to make herself mistress of the Bird, which would inform her of the Singing Tree and Golden Water. He magnified the din of the terrible threatening voices which she would hear on all sides of her, and the great number of black stones alone sufficient to strike terror. He entreated her to reflect that those stones were so many brave gentlemen, so metamorphosed for having omitted to observe the principal condition of success in the perilous undertaking, which was not to look behind them before they had got possession of the cage.

When the dervish had done, the princess replied: 'By what I comprehend from your discourse, the difficulties of succeeding in this affair are: first, the getting up to the cage without being frightened at the terrible din of voices I shall hear; and, secondly, not to look behind me. For this last, I hope I shall be mistress enough of myself to observe it; as to the first, I own that voices, such as you represent them to be, are capable of striking terror into the most undaunted; but as in all enterprises and dangers every one may use stratagem. I desire to know of you if I may use any in one of so great importance.'

'And what stratagem is it you would employ?' said the dervish.

'To stop my ears with cotton,' answered the princess, 'that the voices, however terrible, may make the less impression upon my imagination, and my mind remain free from that disturbance which might cause me to lose the use of my reason.'

'Princess,' replied the dervish, 'of all the persons who have addressed themselves to me for information, I do not know that ever one made use of the contrivance you propose. All I know is that they all perished. If you persist in your design, you may make the experiment. You will be fortunate if it succeeds, but I would advise you not to expose yourself to the danger.'

'My good father,' replied the princess, 'I am sure my precaution will succeed, and am resolved to try the experiment. Nothing remains for me but to know which way I must go, and I conjure you not to deny me that information.'

The dervish exhorted her again to consider well what she was going to do. But finding her resolute, he took out a bowl, and presenting it to her, said: 'Take this bowl, mount your horse again, and when you have thrown it before you, follow it through all its windings, till it stops at the bottom of the mountain; there alight and ascend the hill. Go, you know the rest.'

After the princess had thanked the dervish, and taken her leave of him, she mounted her horse, threw the bowl before her, and followed it till it stopped at the foot of the mountain.

She then alighted, stopped her ears with cotton, and after she had well examined the path leading to the summit began with a moderate pace and walked up with intrepidity. She heard the voices and perceived the great service the cotton was to her. The higher she went, the louder and more numerous the voices seemed, but they were not capable of making any impression upon her. She heard a great many affronting speeches and raillery very disagreeable to a woman, which she only laughed at.

'I mind not,' said she to herself, 'all that can be said, were it worse; I only laugh at them and shall pursue my way.'

At last, she climbed so high that she could perceive the cage and the Bird which endeavoured, in company with the voices, to frighten her, crying in a thundering tone, notwithstanding the smallness of its size: 'Retire, fool, and approach no nearer.'

The princess, encouraged by this sight, redoubled her speed, and by effort gained the summit of the mountain, where the ground was level; then running directly to the cage and clapping her hand upon it, cried: 'Bird, I have you, and you shall not escape me.'

While Periezade was pulling the cotton out of her ears the Bird said to her: 'Heroic princess, be not angry with me for joining with those who exerted themselves to preserve my liberty. Though in a cage, I was content with my condition; but since I am destined to be a slave, I would rather be yours than any other person's, since you have obtained me so courageously. From this instant, I swear entire submission to all your commands. I know who you are. You do not; but the time will come when I shall do you essential service, for which I hope you will think yourself obliged to me. As a proof of my sincerity, tell me what you desire, and I am ready to obey you.'

The princess's joy was the more inexpressible, because the conquest she had made had cost her the lives of two beloved brothers and given her more trouble and danger than she could have imagined.

'Bird,' said she, 'it was my intention to have told you that I wish for many things which are of importance, but I am overjoyed that you have shown your goodwill and prevented me. I have been told that there is not far off a Golden Water, the property of which is very wonderful; before all things, I ask you to tell me where it is.'

The Bird showed her the place, which was just by, and she went and filled a little silver flagon which she had brought with her. She returned at once and said: 'Bird, this is not enough; I want also the Singing Tree; tell me where it is.'

'Turnabout,' said the Bird, 'and you will see behind you a wood where you will find the tree.'

The princess went into the wood, and by the harmonious concert she heard, soon knew the tree among many others, but it was very large and high. She came back again and said: 'Bird, I have found the Singing Tree, but I can neither pull it up by the roots nor carry it.'

The Bird replied: 'It is not necessary that you should take it up; it will be sufficient to break off a branch and carry it to plant in your garden; it will take root as soon as it is put into the earth, and in a little time will grow to as fine a tree as that you have seen.'

When the princess had obtained possession of the three things for which she had conceived so great a desire, she said again: 'Bird, what you have yet done for me is not sufficient. You have been the cause of the death of my two brothers, who must be among the black stones I saw as I ascended the mountain. I wish to take the princes home with me.'

The Bird seemed reluctant to satisfy the princess in this point, and indeed made some difficulty to comply.

'Bird,' said the princess, 'remember you told me that you were my slave. You are so; and your life is in my disposal.'

'That I cannot deny,' answered the bird; 'but although what you now ask is more difficult than all the rest, yet I will do it for you. Cast your eyes around,' added he, 'and look if you can see a little pitcher.'

'I see it already,' said the princess.

'Take it then,' said he, 'and as you descend the mountain, sprinkle a little of the water that is in it upon every black stone.'

The princess took up the pitcher accordingly, carried with her the cage and Bird, the flagon of Golden Water and the branch of the Singing Tree. And as she descended the mountain, she threw a little of the water on every black stone, which was changed immediately into a man. And as she did not miss one stone, all the horses, both of her brothers and of the other gentlemen, resumed their natural forms also. She instantly recognised Bahman and Perviz, as they did her, and ran to embrace her. She returned their embraces and expressed her amazement.

'What do you here, my dear brothers?' said she, and they told her they had been asleep.

'Yes,' replied she, 'and if it had not been for me, perhaps you might have slept till the day of judgment. Do not you remember that you came to fetch the Talking Bird, the Singing Tree and the Golden Water, and did not you see, as you came along, the place covered with black stones? Look and see if there be any now. The gentlemen and their horses who surround us, and you yourselves, were these black stones. If you desire to know how this wonder was performed,' continued she, showing the pitcher, which she set down at the foot of the mountain, 'it was done by virtue of the water which was in this pitcher, with which I sprinkled every stone. After I had made the Talking Bird (which you see in this cage) my slave, by his directions I found out the Singing Tree, a branch of which I have now in my hand;

and the Golden Water, with which this flagon is filled; but being still unwilling to return without taking you with me, I constrained the Bird, by the power I had over him, to afford me the means. He told me where to find this pitcher, and the use I was to make of it.'

The Princes Bahman and Perviz learned by this relation the obligation they had to their sister, as did all the other gentlemen, who expressed to her that, far from envying her happiness in the conquest she had made, and which they all had aspired to, they thought they could not better express their gratitude for restoring them to life again, than by declaring themselves her slaves, and that they were ready to obey her in whatever she should command.

'Gentlemen,' replied the princess, 'if you had given any attention to my words, you might have observed that I had no other intention in what I have done than to recover my brothers; therefore, if you have received any benefit, you owe me no obligation, and I have no further share in your compliment than your politeness toward me, for which I return you my thanks. In other respects, I regard each of you as quite as free as you were before your misfortunes, and I rejoice with you at the happiness which has accrued to you by my means. Let us, however, stay no longer in a place where we have nothing to detain us, but mount our horses and return to our respective homes.'

The princess took her horse, which stood in the place where she had left him. Before she mounted, Prince Bahman desired her to give him the cage to carry.

'Brother,' replied the princess, 'the Bird is my slave, and I will carry him myself. If you will take the pains to carry the branch of the Singing Tree, there it is; only hold the cage while I get on horseback.'

When she had mounted her horse, and Prince Bahman had given her the cage, she turned about and said to Prince Perviz: 'I leave the flagon of Golden Water to your care, if it will not be too much trouble for you to carry it,' and Prince Perviz accordingly took charge of it with pleasure.

When Bahman, Perviz and all the gentlemen had mounted their horses, the princess waited for some of them to lead the way. The two princes paid that compliment to the gentlemen, and they again to the princess, who, finding that none of them would accept the honour, but that it was reserved for her, addressed herself to them and said: 'Gentlemen, I expect that some of you should lead the way.'

To which one who was nearest to her, in the name of the rest, replied: 'Madam, were we ignorant of the respect due to your sex, yet after what you have done for us there is no deference we would not willingly pay you, notwithstanding your modesty; we entreat you no longer to deprive us of the happiness of following you.'

'Gentlemen,' said the princess, 'I do not deserve the honour you do me and accept it only because you desire it.'

At the same time, she led the way, and the two princes and the gentlemen followed.

This illustrious company called upon the dervish as they passed, to thank him for his reception and wholesome advice, which they had all found to be sincere. He was dead, however; whether of old age, or because he was no longer necessary to show the way to obtaining the three rarities, did not appear. They pursued their route but lessened in their numbers every day. The gentlemen who, as we said before, had come from different countries, after severally repeating their obligations to the princess and her brothers, took leave of them one after another as they approached the road by which they had come.

As soon as the princess reached home, she placed the cage in the garden, and the Bird no sooner began to warble than he was surrounded by nightingales, chaffinches, larks, linnets, goldfinches, and every species of birds of the country. The branch of the Singing Tree was no sooner set in the midst of the parterre, a little distance from the house, than it took root and in a short time became a large tree, the leaves of which gave as harmonious a concert as those of the parent from which it was gathered. A large basin of beautiful marble was placed in the garden, and when it was finished, the princess poured into it all the Golden Water from the flagon, which instantly increased and swelled so much that it soon reached up to the edges of the basin, and afterward formed in the middle a fountain twenty feet high, which fell again into the basin perpetually, without running over.

The report of these wonders was presently spread abroad, and as the gates of the house and those of the gardens were shut to nobody, a great number of people came to admire them.

Some days after, when the Princes Bahman and Perviz had recovered from the fatigue of their journey, they resumed their former way of living. And as their usual diversion was hunting, they mounted their horses and went for the first time since their return, not to their own demesne, but two or three leagues from their house. As they pursued their sport, the emperor of Persia came in pursuit of game upon the same ground.

When they perceived, by the number of horsemen in different places, that he would soon be up, they resolved to discontinue their chase, and retire to avoid encountering him; but in the very road they took they chanced to meet him in so narrow a way that they could not retreat without being seen. In their surprise they had only time to alight and prostrate themselves before the emperor, without lifting up their heads to look at him. The emperor, who saw they were as well mounted and dressed as if they had belonged to his court, had a curiosity to see their faces. He stopped and commanded them to rise. The princes rose up and stood before him with an easy and graceful air, accompanied with modest countenances. The emperor took some time to view them before he spoke, and after he had admired their good air and mien, asked them who they were and where they lived.

'Sir,' said Prince Bahman, 'we are the sons of the late intendant of your majesty's gardens and live in a house which he built a little before he died, till we should be fit to serve your majesty and ask of you some employ when opportunity offered.'

'By what I perceive,' replied the emperor, 'you love hunting.'

'Sir,' replied Prince Bahman, 'it is our common exercise, and what none of your majesty's subjects who intend to bear arms in your armies, ought, according to the ancient custom of the kingdom, to neglect.'

The emperor, charmed with so prudent an answer, said: 'Since it is so, I should be glad to see your expertness in the chase; choose your own game.'

The princes mounted their horses again and followed the emperor but had not gone far before they saw many wild beasts together. Prince Bahman chose a lion and Prince Perviz a bear, and pursued them with so much intrepidity that the emperor was surprised. They came up with their game nearly at the same time, and darted their javelins with so much skill and address that they pierced the one the lion and the other the bear so effectually that the emperor saw them fall one after the other. Immediately afterward, Prince Bahman pursued another bear, and Prince Perviz another lion, and killed them in a short time, and would have beaten out for fresh game, but the emperor would not let them, and sent to them to come to him.

When they approached, he said: 'If I had given you leave, you would soon have destroyed all my game; but it is not that which I would preserve, but your persons; for I am so well assured your bravery may one time or other be serviceable to me, that from this moment your lives will be always dear to me.'

The emperor, in short, conceived so great a kindness for the two princes, that he invited them immediately to make him a visit, to which Prince Bahman replied: 'Your majesty does us an honour we do not deserve, and we beg you will excuse us.'

The emperor, who could not comprehend what reason the princes could have to refuse this token of his favour, pressed them to tell him why they excused themselves.

'Sir,' said Prince Bahman, 'we have a sister younger than ourselves, with whom we live in such perfect union, that we undertake nothing before we consult her, nor she anything without asking our advice.'

'I commend your brotherly affection,' answered the emperor. 'Consult your sister, meet me tomorrow, and give me an answer.'

The princes went home but neglected to speak of their adventure in meeting the emperor and hunting with him, and also of the honour he had done them, yet did not the next morning fail to meet him at the place appointed.

'Well,' said the emperor, 'have you spoken to your sister, and has she consented to the pleasure I expect of seeing you?'

The two princes looked at each other and blushed.

'Sir,' said Prince Bahman, 'we beg your majesty to excuse us, for both my brother and I forgot.'

'Then remember today,' replied the emperor, 'and be sure to bring me an answer tomorrow.'

The princes were guilty of the same fault a second time, and the emperor was so good-natured as to forgive their negligence; but to prevent their forgetfulness the third time, he pulled three little golden balls out of a purse and put them into Prince Bahman's bosom.

'These balls,' said he, smiling, 'will prevent your forgetting a third time what I wish you to do for my sake; since the noise they will make by falling on the floor when you undress will remind you, if you do not recollect it before.'

The event happened just as the emperor foresaw; and without these balls the princes had not thought of speaking to their sister of this affair, for as Prince Bahman unloosed his girdle to go to bed the balls dropped on the floor, upon which he ran into Prince Perviz's chamber, when both went into the Princess Periezade's apartment, and after they had asked her pardon for coming at so unseasonable a time, they told her all the circumstances of their meeting the emperor.

The princess was somewhat surprised at this intelligence.

'Your meeting with the emperor,' said she, 'is happy and honourable and may in the end be highly advantageous to you, but it places me in an awkward position. It was on my account, I know, you refused the emperor, and I am infinitely obliged to you for doing so. I know by this that you would rather be guilty of incivility toward the emperor than violate the union we have sworn to each other. You judge right, for if you had once gone you would insensibly have been engaged to devote yourselves to him.

'But do you think it an easy matter absolutely to refuse the emperor what he seems so earnestly to desire? Monarchs will be obeyed in their desires, and it may be dangerous to oppose them; therefore, if to follow my inclination I should dissuade you from obeying him, it may expose you to his resentment, and may render myself and you miserable. These are my sentiments; but before we conclude upon anything let us consult the Talking Bird and hear what he says; he is penetrating, and has promised his assistance in all difficulties.'

The princess sent for the cage, and after she had related the circumstances to the Bird in the presence of her brothers, asked him what they should do in this perplexity.

The Bird answered: 'The princes, your brothers, must conform to the emperor's pleasure, and in their turn invite him to come and see your house.'

'But, Bird,' replied the princess, 'my brothers and I love one another, and our friendship is yet undisturbed. Will not this step be injurious to that friendship?'

'Not at all,' replied the Bird; 'it will tend rather to cement it.'

'Then,' answered the princess, 'the emperor will see me.'

The Bird told her it was necessary he should, and that everything would go better afterward.

Next morning the princes met the emperor hunting, who asked them if they had remembered to speak to their sister. Prince Bahman approached and answered: 'Sir, we are ready to obey you, for we have not only obtained our sister's consent with great ease, but she took it amiss that we should pay her that deference in a matter wherein our duty to your majesty was concerned. If we have offended, we hope you will pardon us.'

'Do not be uneasy,' replied the emperor. 'I highly approve of your conduct and hope you will have the same deference and attachment to my person, if I have ever so little share in your friendship.'

The princes, confounded at the emperor's goodness, returned no other answer but a low obeisance.

The emperor, contrary to his usual custom, did not hunt long that day. Presuming that the princes possessed with equal to their courage and bravery, he longed with impatience to converse with them more at liberty. He made them ride on each side of him, an honour which was envied by the grand vizier, who was much mortified to see them preferred before him.

When the emperor entered his capital, the eyes of the people, who stood in crowds in the streets, were fixed upon the two Princes Bahman and Perviz; and they were earnest to know who they might be.

All, however, agreed in wishing that the emperor had been blessed with two such handsome princes, and said that his children would have been about the same age if the queen had not been so unfortunate as to lose them.

The first thing the emperor did when he arrived at his palace was to conduct the princes into the principal apartments, who praised without affectation the beauty and symmetry of the rooms, and the richness of the furniture and ornaments. Afterward, a magnificent repast was served up, and the emperor made them sit with him, which they at first refused; but finding it was his pleasure, they obeyed.

The emperor, who had himself much learning, particularly in history, foresaw that the princes, out of modesty and respect, would not take the liberty of beginning any conversation. Therefore, to give them an opportunity, he furnished them with subjects all dinnertime. But whatever subject he introduced, they shewed so much wit, judgment, and discernment, that he was struck with admiration.

'Were these my own children,' said he to himself, 'and I had improved their talents by suitable education, they could not have been more accomplished or better informed.'

In short, he took such great pleasure in their conversation, that, after having sat longer than usual, he led them into his closet, where he pursued his conversation with them, and at last said: 'I never supposed that there were among my subjects in the country youths so well brought up, so lively, so capable; and I never was better pleased with any conversation than yours; but it is time now we should relax our minds with some diversion; and as nothing is more capable of enlivening the mind than music, you shall hear a vocal and instrumental concert which may not be disagreeable to you.'

The emperor had no sooner spoken than the musicians, who had orders to attend, entered, and answered fully the expectations the princes had been led to entertain of their abilities. After the concerts, an excellent farce was acted, and the entertainment was concluded by dancers of both sexes.

The two princes, seeing night approach, prostrated themselves at the emperor's feet; and having first thanked him for the favours and honours he had heaped upon them, asked his permission to retire; which was granted by the emperor, who, in dismissing them, said: 'I give you leave to go; but remember, you will be always welcome, and the oftener you come the greater pleasure you will do me.'

Before they went out of the emperor's presence, Prince Bahman said: 'Sir, may we presume to request that your majesty will do us and our sister the honour to pass by our house, and refresh yourself after your fatigue, the first time you take the diversion of hunting in that neighbourhood? It is not worthy of your presence; but monarchs sometimes have vouchsafed to take shelter in a cottage.'

'My children,' replied the emperor, 'your house cannot be otherwise than beautiful and worthy of its owners. I will call and see it with pleasure, which will be the greater for having for my hosts you and your sister, who is already dear to me from the account you give me of the rare qualities with which she is endowed: and this satisfaction I will defer no longer than tomorrow. Early in the morning I will be at the place where I shall never forget that I first saw you. Meet me, and you shall be my guides.'

When the Princes Bahman and Perviz had returned home, they gave the princess an account of the distinguished reception the emperor had given them and told her that they had invited him to do them the honour, as he passed by, to call at their house, and that he had appointed the next day.

'If it be so,' replied the princess, 'we must think of preparing a repast fit for his majesty; and for that purpose, I think it would be proper we should consult the Talking Bird, who will tell us, perhaps, what meats the emperor likes best.'

The princes approved of her plan, and after they had retired, she consulted the Bird alone.

'Bird,' said she, 'the emperor will do us the honour tomorrow to come and see our house, and we are to entertain him; tell us what we shall do to acquit ourselves to his satisfaction.'

'Good mistress,' replied the Bird, 'you have excellent cooks, let them do the best they can. But above all things, let them prepare a dish of cucumbers stuffed full of pearls, which must be set before the emperor in the first course before all the other dishes.'

'Cucumbers stuffed full of pearls!' cried Princess Periezade with amazement; 'surely, Bird, you do not know what you say; it is an unheard-of dish. The emperor may admire it as a piece of magnificence, but he will sit down to eat, and not to admire pearls; besides, all the pearls I possess are not enough for such a dish.'

'Mistress,' said the Bird, 'do what I say, and be not uneasy about what may happen. Nothing but good will follow. As for the pearls, go early tomorrow morning to the foot of the first tree on your right hand in the park, dig under it, and you will find more than you want.'

That night, the princess ordered a gardener to be ready to attend her, and early the next morning led him to the tree which the Bird had told her of, and bade him dig at its foot. When the gardener came to a certain depth, he found some resistance to the spade, and presently discovered a gold box about a foot square, which he showed the princess.

'This,' said she, 'is what I brought you for; take care not to injure it with the spade.'

When the gardener took up the box, he gave it into the princess's hands, who, as it was only fastened with neat little hasps, soon opened it, and found it full of pearls of a moderate size, but equal and fit for the use that was to be made of them. Very well satisfied with having found this treasure, after she had shut the box again, she put it under her arm and went back to the house, while the gardener threw the earth into the hole at the foot of the tree as it had been before.

The Princes Bahman and Perviz, who, as they were dressing themselves in their own apartments, saw their sister in the garden earlier than usual, as soon as they could get out went to her, and met her as she was returning with a gold box under her arm, which much surprised them.

'Sister,' said Bahman, 'you carried nothing with you when we saw you before with the gardener, and now we see you have a golden box; is this some treasure found by the gardener, and did he come and tell you of it?'

'No, brother,' answered the princess, 'I took the gardener to the place where this casket was concealed and showed him where to dig; but you will be more amazed when you see what it contains.'

The princess opened the box, and when the princes saw that it was full of pearls, which, though small, were of great value, they asked her how she came to the knowledge of this treasure.

'Brothers,' said she, 'come with me and I will tell you.'

The princess, as they returned to the house, gave them an account of her having consulted the Bird, as they had agreed she should, and the answer he had given her; the objection she had raised to preparing a dish of cucumbers stuffed full of pearls, and how he had told her where to find this box. The sister and brothers formed many conjectures to penetrate into what the Bird could mean by ordering them to prepare such a dish; but after much conversation, they agreed to follow his advice exactly.

As soon as the princess entered the house, she called for the head cook; and after she had given him directions about the entertainment for the emperor, said to him: 'Besides all this, you must dress an extraordinary dish for the emperor's own eating, which nobody else must have anything to do with besides yourself. This dish must be of cucumbers stuffed with these pearls:' and at the same time she opened him the box and showed him the jewels.

The chief cook, who had never heard of such a dish, started back, and showed his thoughts by his looks; at which the princess, penetrating, said: 'I see you take me to be mad to order such a dish, which one may say with certainty was never made. I know this as well as you; but I am not mad and give you these orders with the most perfect recollection. You must invent and do the best you can and bring me back what pearls are left.'

The cook could make no reply but took the box and retired; and afterward the princess gave directions to all the domestics to have everything in order, both in the house and gardens, to receive the emperor.

Next day, the two princes went to the place appointed, and as soon as the emperor of Persia arrived, the chase began and lasted till the heat of the sun obliged him to leave off. While Prince Bahman stayed to conduct the emperor to their house, Prince Perviz rode before to show the way, and when he came in sight of the house, spurred his horse, to inform the princess that the emperor was approaching; but she had been told by some servants whom she had placed to give notice, and the prince found her waiting ready to receive him.

When the emperor had entered the courtyard and alighted at the portico, the princess came and threw herself at his feet, and the two princes informed him she was their sister and besought him to accept her respects.

The emperor stooped to raise her, and after he had gazed some time on her beauty, struck with her fine person and dignified air, he said: 'The brothers are worthy of the sister, and she worthy of them; since, if I may judge of her understanding by her person, I am not amazed that the brothers would do nothing without their sister's consent; but,' added he, 'I hope to be better acquainted with you, my daughter, after I have seen the house.'

'Sir,' said the princess, 'it is only a plain country residence, fit for such people as we are, who live retired from the great world. It is not to be compared with the magnificent palaces of emperors.'

'I cannot perfectly agree with you in opinion,' said the emperor very obligingly, 'for its first appearance makes me suspect you. However, I will not pass my judgment upon it till I have seen it all; therefore, be pleased to conduct me through the apartments.'

The princess led the emperor through all the rooms except the hall; and, after he had considered them very attentively, and admired their variety,

'My daughter,' said he to the princess, 'do you call this a country house? The finest and largest cities would soon be deserted if all country houses were like yours. I am no longer surprised that you despise the town. Now let me see the garden, which I doubt not is answerable to the house.'

The princess opened a door which led into the garden, and the first object which presented itself to the emperor's view was the golden fountain. Surprised at so rare an object, he asked from whence that wonderful water, which gave so much pleasure to behold, had been procured; where was its source, and by what art it was made to play so high. He said he would presently take a nearer view of it.

The princess then led him to the spot where the harmonious tree was planted; and there the emperor heard a concert, different from all he had ever heard before; and stopping to see where the musicians were, he could discern nobody far or near, but still distinctly heard the music which ravished his senses.

'My daughter,' said he to the princess, 'where are the musicians I hear? Are they underground, or invisible in the air? Such excellent performers will hazard nothing by being seen; on the contrary, they would please the more.'

'Sir,' answered the princess, smiling, 'they are not musicians, but the leaves of the tree your majesty sees before you, which form this concert; and if you will give yourself the trouble to go a little nearer, you will be convinced, and the voices will be the more distinct.'

The emperor went nearer and was so charmed with the sweet harmony that he would never have been tired with hearing it, but that his desire to have a nearer view of the fountain of golden water forced him away.

'Daughter,' said he, 'tell me, I pray you, whether this wonderful tree was found in your garden by chance, or was a present made to you, or have you procured it from some foreign country? It must certainly have come from a great distance, otherwise curious as I am after natural rarities, I should have heard of it. What name do you call it by?'

'Sir,' replied the princess, 'this tree has no other name than that of the Singing Tree and is not a native of this country. It would at present take up too much time to tell your majesty by what adventures it came here; its history is connected with the Golden Water and the Talking Bird, which came to me at the same time, and which your majesty may presently see. But if it be agreeable to your majesty, after you have rested yourself and recovered the fatigue of hunting, which must be the greater because of the sun's intense heat, I will do myself the honour of relating it to you.'

'My daughter,' replied the emperor, 'my fatigue is so well recompensed by the wonderful things you have shown me, that I do not feel it in the least. Let me see the Golden Water, for I am impatient to see and admire afterward the Talking Bird.'

When the emperor came to the Golden Water, his eyes were fixed so steadfastly upon the fountain that he could not take them off. At last, addressing himself to the princess, he said: 'As you tell me, daughter, that this water has no spring or communication, I conclude that it is foreign, as well as the Singing Tree.'

'Sir,' replied the princess, 'it is as your majesty conjectures; and to let you know that this water has no communication with any spring, I must inform you that the basin is one entire stone, so that the water cannot come in at the sides or underneath. But what your majesty will think most wonderful is that all this water proceeded but from one small flagon, emptied into this basin, which increased to the quantity you see, by a property peculiar to itself, and formed this fountain.'

'Well,' said the emperor, going from the fountain, 'this is enough for one time. I promise myself the pleasure to come and visit it often; but now let us go and see the Talking Bird.'

As he went toward the hall, the emperor perceived a prodigious number of singing birds in the trees around, filling the air with their songs and warblings, and asked why there were so many there and none on the other trees in the garden.

'The reason, sir,' answered the princess, 'is because they come from all parts to accompany the song of the Talking Bird, which your majesty may see in a cage in one of the windows of the hall we are approaching; and if you attend, you will perceive that his notes are sweeter than those of any of the other birds, even the nightingale's.'

The emperor went into the hall; and as the Bird continued singing, the princess raised her voice, and said, 'My slave, here is the emperor, pay your compliments to him.'

The Bird left off singing that instant, when all the other birds ceased also, and said: 'The emperor is welcome; God prosper him and prolong his life!'

As the entertainment was served on the sofa near the window where the Bird was placed, the sultan replied, as he was taking his seat: 'Bird, I thank you, and am overjoyed to find in you the sultan and king of birds.'

As soon as the emperor saw the dish of cucumbers set before him, thinking they were prepared in the best manner, he reached out his hand and took one; but when he cut it, was in extreme surprise to find it stuffed with pearls.

'What novelty is this?' said he; 'and with what design were these cucumbers stuffed thus with pearls, since pearls are not to be eaten?'

He looked at his hosts to ask them the meaning when the Bird interrupting him, said: 'Can your majesty be in such great astonishment at cucumbers stuffed with pearls, which you see with your own eyes, and yet so easily believe that the queen – your wife – gave birth to a dog, a cat, and a piece of wood?'

'I believed those things,' replied the emperor, 'because the attendants assured me of the facts.'

'Those attendants, sir,' replied the Bird, 'were the queen's two sisters, who, envious of her happiness in being preferred by your majesty before them, to satisfy their envy and revenge, have abused your majesty's credulity. If you interrogate them, they will confess their crime. The two brothers and the sister whom you see before you are your own children, whom they exposed, and who were taken in by the intendant of your gardens, who provided nurses for them, and took care of their education.'

This speech presently cleared up the emperor's understanding.

'Bird,' cried he, 'I believe the truth which you discover to me. The inclination which drew me to them told me plainly they must be of my own blood. Come then, my sons, come, my daughter, let me embrace you, and give you the first marks of a father's love and tenderness.'

The emperor then rose, and after having embraced the two princes and the princess, and mingled his tears with theirs, said: 'It is not enough, my children; you must embrace each other, not as the children of the intendant of my gardens, to whom I have been so much obliged for preserving your lives, but as my own children, of the royal blood of the monarchs of Persia, whose glory, I am persuaded you will maintain.'

After the two princes and princess had embraced mutually with new satisfaction, the emperor sat down again with them, and finished his meal in haste; and when he had done, said: 'My children, you see in me your father; tomorrow I will bring the queen, your mother, therefore prepare to receive her.'

The emperor afterward mounted his horse and returned with expedition to his capitol. The first thing he did, as soon as he had alighted and entered his palace, was to command the grand vizier to seize the queen's two sisters. They were taken from their houses separately, convicted, and condemned to death; which sentence was put in execution within an hour.

In the meantime, the Emperor Kosrouschah, followed by all the lords of his court who were then present, went on foot to the door of the great mosque; and after he had taken the queen out of the strict confinement she had languished under for so many years, embracing her in the miserable condition to which she was then reduced, said to her with tears in his eyes: 'I come to entreat your pardon for the injustice I have done you, and to make you the reparation I ought; which I have begun, by punishing the unnatural wretches who put the abominable cheat upon me; and I hope you will look upon it as complete, when I present to you two accomplished princes and a lovely princess, our children. Come and resume your former rank, with all the honours which are your due.'

All this was done and said before great crowds of people who flocked from all parts at the first news of what was passing, and immediately spread the joyful intelligence through the city.

Next morning early the emperor and queen, whose mournful humiliating dress was changed for magnificent

135

robes, went with all their court to the house built by the intendant of the gardens, where the emperor presented the Princes Bahman and Perviz, and the Princess Periezade to their enraptured mother.

'These, much injured wife,' said he, 'are the two princes your sons, and the princess your daughter; embrace them with the same tenderness I have done, since they are worthy both of me and you.'

The tears flowed plentifully down their cheeks at these tender embraces, especially the queen's, from the comfort and joy of having two such princes for her sons, and such a princess for her daughter, on whose account she had so long endured the severest afflictions.

The two princes and the princess had prepared a magnificent repast for the emperor and queen and their court. As soon as that was over, the emperor led the queen into the garden, and showed her the Harmonious Tree and the beautiful effect of the Golden Fountain. She had seen the Bird in his cage, and the emperor had spared no panegyric in his praise during the repast.

When there was nothing to detain the emperor any longer, he took horse, and with the Princes Bahman and Perviz on his right hand, and the queen consort and the princess at his left, preceded and followed by all the officers of his court, according to their rank, returned to his capital. Crowds of people came out to meet them, and with acclamations of joy ushered them into the city, where all eyes were fixed not only upon the queen, and her royal children, but also upon the Bird, which the princess carried before her in his cage, admiring his sweet notes, which had drawn all the other birds about him, and followed him flying from tree to tree in the country, and from one house top to another in the city.

The Princes Bahman and Perviz and the Princess Periezade were at length brought to the palace with pomp, and nothing was to be seen or heard all that night but illuminations and rejoicings both in the palace and in the utmost parts of the city, which lasted many days, and were continued throughout the empire of Persia, as intelligence of the joyful event reached the several provinces.

From: The Arabian Nights: Their Best-known Tales

Finis

Workbooks From The Scheherazade Foundation

We hope that you have enjoyed this collection of stories, gleaned from varying cultural corners of the world, and that you have been entertained by them.

But, have you considered the deeper meanings and interwoven layers that lie hidden beneath the surface?

At The Scheherazade Foundation, we believe that Teaching-Stories contain wisdom, information, and marvels that have the power to transform the way we think, and thereby change our lives.

Employed as a bedrock of culture throughout the centuries – challenging established patterns of thinking, while passing on knowledge and values – tales such as the ones contained in this volume are a rich resource ready and waiting to be mined.

As an aid to help in the perception of less-obvious facets and layers, we have created a series of original Workbooks. Aimed at stimulating thought-provoking discussions and igniting deep reflection, these tools will assist in unlocking the power of Teaching-Stories.